THRIFT STORE PUZZLES

JOHN BODEN

DEAD
SKY
PUBLISHING

Published by Dead Sky Publishing, LLC

Miami Beach, Florida

www.deadskypublishing.com

Cover by Matthew Revert

Design & Formatting by Apparatus Revolution, LLC

Edited by Anna Kubik

Dedicated to several missing pieces:

John Bankes
Clifford Eagle
David Eagle Sr.
Ronald Weldon
Jay Wilburn
Dave Thomas

1

"I know what you're going to say when I tell you that I am two hundred and forty-six years old. You'll roll your eyes, smirk, perhaps, probably with your arms folded at your chest, and think to yourself *'the old boy's cheese has slid quite a distance from his cracker.'*

"Well, then the joke's on you, as I haven't kept my cheese or cracker in the same place for a long, long while. I am Vestus Addison Schmoyer, and I'm as old as independence. I slid from my mother's womb just days before the great document was signed, while the streets of Philadelphia were glut with the joyous cavorting, wrapped in a drapery of rapturous song, the ushering in of a broad-shouldered new period of living.

While the newly dressed nation was unfurling fresh, wet wings, I was suckling a scabrous teat in the dank hold of a marooned fishing boat, stranded on the mucky shore of the septic Delaware river. My mother spent my first moments swatting away rats that were just as famished as her mewling son. As I fed, she wept and watched the fat, furred creatures devour the cord and afterbirth she'd kicked to the side after cutting me free of fleshy shackle with a rusted sliver of tin. The squeals of the rats and I were an indecipherable chorus that lulled my sweet mother to permanent sleep. Her blood pooled beneath us like a warm slippery quilt. Red as life, it was. The rats went to work on the poor woman and left me to sleep in her lap.

It was there I would be found by a young fisherman, Barton Gand, the following morning, when he would notice a stream of bloated rats leaving the vessel in a pulsating line. Would note the faint flicker of candlelight through the broken boards of the hull. Would lift me from the gory crib of my mother and carry me out into the bleary eyed world. I suppose I ought to hate him for that..."

"I wasn't aware that one day, the vermin and I would be kin. Siblings in tenacity and resilience. A coal black vein threading us together and to the moon as though we were the tail of a terrific midnight kite."

The old man stopped speaking, and with a slightly shaking finger, wiped the dollop of spittle from the corner of his mouth. He smiled and nodded his head quickly, a mimicry of a bow.

2

"Man, oh man, Ken, I get chills every time you do that. I mean, I know you wrote it and all, but so long ago and you just recite it as though it's fact. Like you're remembering your kid's high school graduation or your wedding day or something."

The old man winced a little at those comparisons, but the young nurse fellow was smiling so big, his hairy cheeks could barely cage it and he did not notice. Tierny looked over at the boy, who was also smiling but slightly shaking his head in either embarrassment or indifference. He'd heard this before, several times.

The old man smiled, then finished drinking from his cup. He sat it on the table beside the worn copy of *Midnight Rictus,* the only book that had ever brought Ken Allenwood acclaim and a somewhat steady income. The only one still mentioned on lists and horror fanzine write ups, mostly due to the wretched film version that came about decades earlier. Ken was not bitter though; the checks had cleared and had paid for the necessary things. He had written the novel, and he had the story in him, as much as his spine and heart. Whatever the movie studio people did or didn't do with it, mattered nil. He picked up the book and looked at the cover with fondness. The black matte painted night sky was broken only by the hint of a smile made up of many small points.

"I signed it for you, I even used the fountain pen that I wrote the original longhand draft with all those years ago."

With a trembling hand, he held it out to the nurse who took it gingerly.

"Well, Tierny, let me tell you where I learned to read publicly. I learned from one of the very best back when I was first coughing words onto the page. His name was Robert Denial, and because the world is an unjust place, a cruel place, he never seemed to claw his way to the ranks of the biggies. His fans are ferocious in their loyalty though. Every single book he eked into the world is gold. Look him up next time you're at the library. Ol' Bob was a gentle man, a smile that could cover any wound or occasion. The warmest, he was. To watch him do a reading was like watching a one man play by a consummate actor. He stalked the room, no regard for size, and looked every person in the eye, then personally took them by the hand, and led them into his territory. He almost never read from a book or page, choosing to memorize the material and deliver it as though mining from memory. I've watched him reduce them to tears or provoke riotous laughter; he held them all right in the palm of his fucking hand, I tell you. An absolute master, he was. A beautiful soul."

"Is he still writing?" The question came from Tierny.

"Sadly, no. He left us many years ago. His demons got the reins, I fear. Left him along the soul road, chewed up by the world and spat out as gristle. That's what it does, you know. Eats and swallows and regurgitates...over and over, forever. Fucking tragedy."

At the second use of the explicit curse, the boy chuckled low, nearly under his breath, and turned the page of his monster magazine. He looked up and the old man gave him a wink. Elijah nodded even though his mind was beginning to wander, as it usually did. Tierny was still smiling at both the man and the boy, but his mouth was not matched by his eyes. They held a slight sadness. Tierny knew that this was just a longer pocket of clarity in a sea of befuddlement and confusion that would grow deeper and choppier over the coming months. He'd watched it devour many and would see it masticate many more. He held the book close to his chest, thought of the old man carefully exacting his signature on the first page for him. He would hold it as treasure for the rest of his days, and though something sharp jabbed his heart, he kept the smile on for both of them.

3
_____

Ken was having a good day today.

A clear day. An *On point* day. Now, at least. The rest of the day seemed up in the air.

When Elijah had come over earlier, just before lunch but after his mother had left for her shift at the factory, Ken was sitting in the recreation room. It was really just a big room with three couches, a chair, a TV on the wall, and plenty of space for wheelchair parking, and for walkers poised at the ready.

Ken was in the large recliner closest to the wall, his head tipped back with his eyes mostly closed. Elijah had watched him sleep for long minutes, watched his eyes roll beneath the thin lids. He slowly and calmly rested a hand on the old man's forearm and gently squeezed.

"Mr. Ken?" He whispered.

Ken's eyes popped open in surprise, but he didn't jump or cry out. He looked at the boy for a few seconds, the lack of knowledge as to who he was, glaringly apparent. His brow furrowed in dark confusion, but then, the wrinkles there began to smooth out and a warm recognition blossomed in his expression. His thin lips rose in a smile and his bony hand found the boy's, still on his arm. Ken's skin was so thin and cool, Elijah thought, as he rubbed his thumb over the old man's. It was a comforting gesture; his mother had done it when he was a little boy, scared by something and unable to sleep. He figured this whole dementia thing must be terrifying for Ken, so he did what he could.

"It means his brain is slowing and breaking down, kiddo. It means a lot more than that and a lot more details than I can even go into but the gum of it is that. Old Ken is losing things. Little things now and then but, eventually, all of it. He won't recall anyone or much of anything. It's like a puzzle from the thrift store, there are pieces missing and no matter how much time and attention you give it, it will never be complete."

Tierny had told Elijah that weeks earlier. He had just crossed the street from his house and was making his way to the facility's side entrance when he heard Tierny whistle. The bearded man had been out under the willow tree sneaking a smoke. He said he had to tell him something because he knew he liked to visit Ken and listen to his stories and keep the man company. He had leaned over to look the boy in the eye, a courtesy most adults never bothered to extend, and laid it on him.

Elijah wasn't a little kid. He was thirteen and four months. He was not as tall as his peers, but he knew that would change one day. His mother had promised him, and that woman never told a lie. He knew what was tragic when he heard it. He knew sadness well, and when he felt tears broadcasting the news about his elderly friend, he felt no shame in them.

Tierny went on to explain, in his matter-of-fact way, that what this all meant was that eventually Ken would not remember Elijah. He wouldn't be able to place his face or

Tierny's or Nurse Paula's or anyone else's who saw him every day. He'd forget his own face and history. A glimpse in the mirror would be a window to a grizzled stranger. His beloved stories would become pages torn from a bizarre book, written in a foreign language. He would just fade, one memory or function at a time, until he was gone. Essentially disappeared.

"He'll disappear." Tierny had said, as he sucked the cigarette between his fingers down to the end. He bared his teeth like some woodland beast, smoke leaking from between them. His eyes were wet with tired tears. Elijah felt his throat fill with something thick.

His eyes promised more of their own salt water. He nodded and slipped inside, leaving Tierny in his cove of whispering shade to feed his lungs their shadows.

"Oh hello, boy." The old man spoke, his usually clear and commanding voice fragile in that moment with phlegm and age.

"And I beg you, *plead* even...drop the Mister jazz." They both chuckled then.

4

I t was the following Tuesday and Tierny had gone to finish his rounds, to deliver meds and meals. Ken Allenwood sat at the small round table by the entrance to the hallway and poked his Jello with a fork. The square of yellow gelatin swayed and bobbed in response.

"Vile stuff," the old man muttered and twisted his lips into a grimace.

"I used to like Jello, but then I watched this show on how they make it and...yuck, no thanks." Elijah grimaced as he spoke.

"It's all the matter deemed not good enough for hot dogs and that, my boy, speaks volumes." Ken poked again and the dessert waggled.

"I'm glad I'm full enough from the sandwich."

"Sandwich good then? I like to put potato chips on my sandwiches."

"I believe I'll have you make my sandwiches from now on. *That* was two slices of almost stale bread, a spittle of yellow mustard and some type of processed cheese. I shall be thankful when I forget how to be disappointed."

He chuckled and put down his fork, then wiped his hands on the cloth napkin in his lap. He smiled at Elijah, who smiled back. "So, it's been, what, three days since I've seen you? My how you've grown, son."

The old man winked again. He was taking the piss, Elijah knew. He had told Ken previously how he hated being small for his age, much smaller than the other kids, and Ken had told him that stature rarely had anything to do with weights and measures. He'd seen giants who were infantile and ants who were gargantuan. He had an easy way of soothing the boy's many worries. Elijah was in danger of being lost in his own head again when the old man tapped his ring on the table edge. The boy looked at him.

"I think I'd like to go out into the world today, Elijah. Drink some of that sweet country air." The old man stood and extended his arm for the young man to take. The pair of them carefully made their way to the side door, after a pause at the nurse's station desk to gain permission from nurse Holly to go out to the bench. She was less perky than usual, which suited them fine, and she gave the patented "*Be careful, don't go anywhere but the bench*" speech. They agreed and propped the big door open with the statue of the owl that sat there for just such a purpose.

The old man said the outer door, squeaked the language of haunted houses and Ken's description made Elijah smile. He sure knew his way to the kid's horror loving heart. A road stippled with vampires and werewolves, paved with aliens and amorphous creatures. Beastly blacktop and cobblestone critters.

The old man and the boy were family, brought together by mutual interests but bound by a necessity. The old man, devoid of any living kin, and the boy, with a yawning chasm where his father once was, and where his mother simply could not be. Nobody wanted to be alone, especially those who clearly state the opposite. *'The biggest lies are those we tell ourselves,'* Ken had once told him. It made so much sense that Elijah had written it down in the margin of his battered *EERIE* magazine.

Any book is a bible if it guides, balms, bribes and belittles.

5

A big crow picked at something dead in the high grass along the road. Neither Ken nor Elijah could see what it was, but the bird and the aura of flies informed them of its presence. The bird dipped its beak into the weeds and grass and raised its head, pulling a thick strand of something free from the mystery carcass. It took flight and after a brief stopover on the *Welcome to Cordry* sign at the edge of the ditch, disappeared into the branches of the large willow tree that marked the middle of the yard of the home. Elijah laughed and the old man turned to face him.

"No secret humor, young man." He faux scolded.

"That crow seemed happier with his nasty roadkill than you were with your cheese sandwich." The boy tried to stifle his laugh but failed.

"I don't see the levity in that. We don't laugh at tragic events."

Ken held a dire expression as long as he could before he too, cracked and fell into laughter.

The pair calmed themselves and resumed sitting in the

cool air, watching the clouds slide across the sky. The sun was muted by a haze that telegraphed possible rain later.

"Ken?"

"Yes."

"You don't really think you're a vampire, do you?"

"Who says I'm thinking?" The old man raised an eyebrow and smiled at his young companion. The boy just stared at him; a look of concern woven across his features.

"I certainly do not. I'm not insane, boy. I mean I probably am but no more than you or Tierny or your mom or anyone. Sanity is of degrees and most of us operate a few map lines away from it. I never said I was a vampire. I have never said much of anything other than that I am very old. Very."

"But the way you do your thing where you recall from your book. You aren't just reciting from memory. You're like, reliving it. Like in a trance or something. I asked Tierny and he said that happens with people..."

"People my age? Yes, it does. The threads that hold the pages of our mind together begin to pull away, the glue dries and flakes and they fall free, landing on the floor with our real memories and histories. Elijah, I never drank anyone's blood. I don't fly or crawl or turn into a bat or a dog or anything. I'm not carved out of shadow, and I don't sizzle away in the daytime. Garlic won't kill me, but the heartburn it delivers may as well. I have just outlived anyone that ever meant anything to me." He paused, considering the sting of what just slipped past his lips, and nodded at the boy.

"Mostly anyone. I have made new friends that I love as dearly as long lost family."

"I know all of those things are bullshit. But I also know, my mom said, that all legends are like pearls. They start with a grain of sandy truth."

"Your mother is a smart woman and bless her tired heart for raising you the same. Son, I am just as I have said, I am very old. *Very.* I have lived as long as the sum of several life spans. Am I a supernatural creature? No. I don't really think so. Am I immortal? I think not. Death will come for me as any other, just at a slower pace."

"Will you tell me about your life? The real stuff, not your book?"

The old man's smile was a wilted lily on parchment. His eyes drifted a bit, and he took in a small breath.

"One day, perhaps."

"Just one thing. Tell me one real thing from your life."

"I shall tell you the very first thing. Told to me by my mother when I visited her during her last days. She had what they called the consumption. It seemed to be as common as cancer now. I suppose it always was, just earned itself a shorter name, if not more accurate. I was born on the edge of nowhere, a sprawling place on what would become the edge of the state of Ohio. Anyway, I was meant to be a pair."

"My twin and I were born minutes apart. Mother named him Vestus after an uncle. He slid into the world but never managed to court a breath. Some type of deformity. His skull never came together correctly, an oversized oral cavity that practically cleaved the skull in two. It... he actually had several teeth. My mother wouldn't touch him, hold him, or even look upon him. My heart hurt for him when I heard that. To grow inside of someone, to be nurtured and lulled by a body only to have that very one shun ye upon appearance. Ultimate heartbreak, I'd wager. The doctor was poised to throw him on the fire, but my grandmother stopped him. She was of the mountain people. She knew secrets that aren't spoken of in the light of the sun. Polite way to say it.

The old woman cradled the tiny body in her arms for an hour, they said."

Ken paused as if to consider how far to go with this tale. He licked his dry lips and looked at the expression on the boy's face, his young attention span being held prisoner, and went on.

"She put her mouth almost to his and spoke to him, *into* him, sang softly and whispered prayers, no one was really certain to whom, and then the woman drew a deep breath. She removed from her dress pocket a small green bottle from which she poured the contents onto the floor and then pursed her lips to the opening. Tears streamed down her wrinkled cheeks as she exhaled the breath into that glass vessel and capped it quickly. She secreted the bottle back into her pocket and handed the body of my cold, blue brother to the doctor then she left the house. My mother said she heard the door slam and happened to glance out the window by the bed, her eyes drowsed, her body aching and worn. She swore she saw the old woman stop and stare up above the window. Probably at the black oily smoke that climbed from the chimney. The woman smiled and nodded and walked towards the woods, my mother said. She told me that Grandma was not seen again for years."

The boy looked at the man and waited to see if he would continue, pulling back the curtain to reveal more details of his life, more of this bizarre yarn he just started. But he could see the weariness in his friend's face.

"You didn't have a dad?" Elijah asked.

"Of course, I did. I never met the man. He was killed before my birth. It was always my mother and I. Until I moved on and away. And then just me...for a long, long lifetime."

"But you were married. Did you have any children?"

"I was married a few times. I have outlived all my wives." Ken replied with a distance in his voice, completely side-stepping the second part of the boy's query. Elijah picked up on it but didn't press the issue.

"So, you named the main vampire in your book after him, your brother." Elijah said. It was a statement begging confirmation, not so much a question. The old man nodded.

"I never knew him in life, so I decided to make a life with him, *for* him, in words. And I made him a monster."

"It was just made up. Just a story and you named a character after him."

"Absence makes the heart grow angry, boy, and anger is a most fertile womb."

"Why would you be angry, it had nothing to do with you?"

"Not me, I wasn't ever the angry one." He turned his face up toward the sky and allowed the warmth from the sun to touch him, to pinch his tired eyes to slits.

"Nothing so stalwart as thee that is devoid of life, denied of breath yet held up as shield and bow by those that run beneath the hooded eyes of God." The old man almost mumbled the words, but Elijah heard.

"Where is that from?" The boy pressed.

Ken didn't answer or elaborate, just kept his eyes closed and enjoyed the tranquil environment.

Elijah grew bored, but not wanting to waste time with his friend, he slid a worn comic book out from the knee pocket of his cargo shorts.

As he started reading, laughter floated in the air like birds, and he looked up to see several boys riding along the edge of the road on their bikes. They were all around his age, yet he couldn't assign a name to them if he had to. To them, he was a ghost in the cemetery of their existence. He just wandered their dusty halls and once in a while, they sensed him, they looked through him, but mostly they denied his occupancy in their space. He felt the flutter in his chest when he thought overlong about his loneliness. He returned his gaze to the comic in his hand and hoped that maybe one day it would be different.

6

B y the time he had finished the second tale in the comic, Ken was softly snoring. Elijah looked at the man for a long while. He chewed on his bottom lip as he considered Ken. He seemed sharper the last few visits. Elijah worked a tiny piece of skin from the inside of his mouth as he wondered how many years and memories were melting away in his head while he slept. He imagined a great bladed contraption mowing through a hall lined with stacks of books, the hungry and eager blades chewing through the collected recollections of a long lifetime. Reducing them to shreds, and those shreds to pulp. He pushed the thought away before giving his attention back to the Crypt Creep and his fearsome fables.

The afternoon crawled on in a slender train of quiet, only broken by the occasional car engine or loud holler from a child playing somewhere. It was about an hour and half later when Holly poked her head out and told them to come in. The district manager was possibly enroute and if they were caught being this lax about things, *heads would roll*, was the exact phrase she used.

Elijah gently shook the old man to rouse him. He stood and held his arm out for Ken to steady himself upon standing. The old man had a tiny drop of drool on his chin, but the boy didn't have the heart to tell him just then. It would embarrass him. They made their way back inside and the kid helped Ken to his room, where he practically fell into the comfy chair and had the boy turn on the radio that sat on the dresser. Voices spoke low, almost inaudibly. That's how Ken liked it. Within a few minutes the voices stopped, and Rosemary Clooney started asking them to *Come On- A My House*.

"Mr. Ken, I'm going to go home across the street and have my dinner. I can come back over after if you want. If not, I'll just watch a movie and go to bed early. All this doing nothing wears a body down."

"Boy, doesn't it?" The old man answered, then raised an eyebrow and turned his mouth down to a frown stance. "And what have I told you about the Mister business?"

"To cut it out. Sorry, Ma raised me to be mannerly."

"And that you are. You're a very kind boy, wasting so much of your fresh years with an old bat like me. I'm honored and happy to have you around. It's been a very long life and the bulk of it, it seems, I've been alone. Mostly by choice, but solitary is a lonely word and a very large place to be. The only voice is yours and you know what you're going to say. The years are just an endless chain of repeated actions. Tedious."

"But you were famous. You wrote books and created worlds."

"Ha. Sounds glamorous when you say it like that, but the truth is, no one cares. Oh sure, they'll buy the book and love the tale, but they tend to forget the one who created it. I mean, there are authors who are huge and have armies of frothing fans. Wear an armor of accolades. Most, however, will never be recognizable by face or manner. They write in near anonymity, backs breaking under the pressure of dancing for the world under the stones of apathy. I sound bitter. I'm not. We do it not for fame, but for the same reason a fish swims or a bird flies, what the hell else would it do?"

"I get it. It's sort of like a clown, like Bozo. He was famous but if he walked into a room without the face paint and wig and all, no one would know him from a can of hairspray, would they?"

"Odd analogy, but yes. It's close to that."

"I'll see you. I can come back later, Ken." Elijah picked up the worn canvas satchel he had hung over the knob of the door. He pulled aside the flap and slid his comic book in to mingle with the other contents, then pulled the strap over his shoulder and stood beside the old man, who still stared.

"No, but thank you all the same. You've hitched your wagon to this weary ass long enough today. Go eat your lovingly prepared food. Watch one of those horror films you love so dearly. Screaming large-breasted girlies and deadly gardening tools." Ken chuckled but it faded fast. The old man stared at the dresser, *through* it, most likely into that realm where he hid his thoughts from the invisible bandit that was stealing them. His eyes narrowed in focus, his mouth opening slightly.

"Okay. Have a good evening, I'll see you tomorrow. I'll bring you lunch. I'll clear it with Holly on the way out."

Ken nodded but did not break eye contact with whatever was holding it. The boy slipped out and was gone.

~

KEN SLOWLY TURNED and looked at the spot where the kid had been standing, listened to the far away sound of Elijah's voice and the higher voice of Nurse Holly. He could not make out exact words, but he heard the woman laugh and Elijah follow with his own. He heard the door squeak, followed by the outer one slamming closed. He sighed through thin lips and went back to looking at the spot above the dresser, while his mind showed him things he still recalled. Things he held close and secure from the robbing leech that had latched onto him.

The years flowed by as water. Brackish and muddied at times, clear as tears at others, slowing when the desired memory came into view.

Vestus stands on the banks of the river and watches the large boat with its wheel churning a wake to follow. The sun is dipping behind the mountains and the sky, that special color of deep bruising. The water beyond the turning paddles of the boat shimmers like the glass of a midnight mirror. He sees the women on the deck, dancing and laughing, wrapped in satins and gauze. Their robust figures in lighter colored garments cutting through the arriving darkness. Vestus pinpoints his target and smiles, the points of his many teeth flashing like a new blade. His belly longs for a brunette tonight and he shall do his best to accommodate. He licks thin lips and pulls his coat tight over his slim figure. He flips up the collar and hears it whoosh softly against his beard. His long fingers tucked into the waist pockets of the jacket. He begins the walk down the hillside to the dock, the very place the boat is pulling into. He waits next to the wooden plank that is slid into place to bridge the boat to land. He does not move or speak until the object of his desire comes down the ramp. Her dark curls bounce against her bare shoulders. Her pale skin shines like milk. He holds out a hand for her to take and steady herself as she reaches the bottom. She looks into his eyes and while she does not seem to recognize him, she takes his hand, and he helps her down onto the dock.

"Thank you, kind sir." she says, her voice breathy and thin.

"Most welcome, my lady. May I escort you to wherever it is you're going? It is growing dark and I fret for your safety in this setting." He stabs a smile onto the end of the sentence, and she opens her mouth in slight surprise. "I'm only going over to the hotel but you may, and I thank you." She curtsies.

Vestus nods and the couple walk, slowly, down the length of the dock, in the direction of the hotel that squats at the river end of the town. In the coming days, witnesses will attest that they saw her get off the boat and walk towards her lodging. They will be correct in their description of her attire and appearance. They will accurately note the time of evening. Where the infant moon was. But not one, will give mention to the handsome tall fellow who met her at the ramp and escorted her to town. No one will recall anything but seeing her alive both on and off the boat until she was discovered dead in the alley beside the hotel as the new morning sun yawned in the sky. A deep second smile gaping beneath her chin, barely drooling precious red.

A blink. A shimmery transition as though looking through heat rising from a desert highway. There is a woman standing by a creek. It is his beautiful Ava. Her dress is winter bright, and she clutches a small bouquet of purple and blue flowers close to her chest. Vestus–no, Ken– watches her. Pins her image to the cork of his mind as though it were a captured butterfly. Takes in her beauty. His eyes are practically choking, his mouth can do nothing but smile. This creature said 'yes' and in minutes their lives will be a knot. One that no fury of fingers can undo. His chest hurts from the fevered beating of his heart. It stretches with every pulsing throb to accommodate the joy he feels.

Another blink. Ken sits beside the bed and watches the husk, what remains of the woman he wed, the one he has loved these long years, his Ava, sleep. Her drawn mouth wheezes, whispers her breaths, and her closed lids flutter like an evening moth. Her bony chest rises almost imperceptibly. He sees the one small swell of her remaining breast and the dam breaks. So strong she was—is—has always been. She lost that breast to cancer nearly thirty-six years earlier. He looked into those pale blue eyes that now look like pearl onions, and felt nothing was beyond his doing. He has had almost sixty-six years with this treasure, and knows he will soon bury her as such. His hand finds the desiccated thing that is hers, gives it a small squeeze and lets the heavy tears fall when he receives nothing in return. He does what he always does, whispers apologies, and promises that feel like eely lies.

Ken Allenwood gasped and blinked his eyes rapidly as he dragged himself from the mire of his memories and as soon as he realized where he was, and that he was alone, he softly wept.

Holly slipped into her denim jacket and pulled the scrunchie from her hair, allowing the long brown curls to fall over her shoulders. She dragged her stubby fingers through the mess to loosely comb it. Her bracelets jingled like the tags on a dog's collar. Paula stood beside the chair, still taking off her own sweater. Holly grabbed her keys from the drawer and pushed it closed as she stepped out from behind the station counter.

"So glad that asshole never stopped by. I mean, we were pretty much on point. I wrangled old Ken inside and the boy went home. Tierny is off today. Those are the three things likely to get us a reprimand or worse from Mr. Strayer, *if* he stops by. It made me sad a little, they're like a little adopted family."

"Elijah is never a bother, and the old man loves him. I think they're good for one another. And Ken has no family at all. The boy only has his mom, and she works so much. And Tierny is his, what is it, Uncle-in-law? Cousin? That *by marriage* shit confuses me. I get that we aren't a babysitting business, but he doesn't hurt anything and what's it cost us?

Maybe an extra lunch once in a while." Paula replied, a tad more defensively than intended.

Holly just kept going, with no indication she took offense. Holly's fingers fretted over one of the buttons on her jacket. A band where the guys looked like girls and the music had huge choruses and guitar solos.

"I hear you, but the district manager wouldn't like it, you know he wouldn't. We run things pretty loose. We're a small town and light volume, but we still have to put on the right suit when he drops by. I know I can't afford to lose this job."

"Sadly, true. Well, I've got things under control here, Holly. Overnight it is usually pretty laid back. I sit and read and once an hour walk the hall and poke my head in each room. Then come back and read some more."

"Yeah. Okay. I'm outta here if I wanna stop by Prettyman's drugstore before they close and grab some foam insoles for these damn shoes. I might grab something to eat, go home and to bed. Do not pass go, do not collect two hundred dollars."

The two of them laughed and Paula went to work on her book, while Holly exited via the squeaking door. Holly looked up to the moon and thought it almost had a face with the way the darker clouds were slowly hanging in front of it. Almost looked like a skull. She introduced a cigarette to her red lips and produced a lighter from her jacket pocket. It had a brightly colored bass on it, leaping at a fly. It was a ridiculous thing, that had been her mother's. A small theft from a cluttered side table while the home care nurses were clearing the bedding, and the funeral men were bagging their cargo. It still spit a flame on the first flick five years later. Holly frowned, smoke leaking from where her lips held the cigarette, and got into her Mazda. After two attempts to start it, Holly got it running and drove off.

9

He smelled dead leaves composting in the shady gulleys of the woods. Moldering piles beside boulders and against windfall mounds. As he slept, his nostrils flared, and his eyelids twitched. He heard the crunch of the forest floor under his booted feet. Heard his walking stick tap against stone and trunk as he ambled by. His heart stammered as he felt a longing for his simpler life in the woods. His shack and his puttering around to fill the void of the days. Back when he had a name. Back when he was Randall. Before he could settle too comfortably into memories of his old self and ways, they were plucked from behind his eyes. Icy dark fingers pulling them like a strip of film from a projector. The roommate in his head cackled and laughed and what little identity was left in the man was stomped like campfire ashes beneath calloused soles.

The old trailer was baking. It was humid and dank. Like a barn. The Mouth awoke in a slick sheen of oily sweat. The cloth that swaddled him was damp and sour. His sleeping bag was like a chrysalis. He would wriggle down into it every morning as the sun was a bright tongue licking the edge of the horizon, and zip himself into a pocket of darkness. He would not emerge again until the same sun was retreating like a scared pup.

Sometimes there was no visible change, he emerged the same as when he got in, but other times, a monster slid from the acrylic bedding. It wore his face and body but the eyes that met him in the mirror were not his own. The mind behind those eyes thought differently than his everyday brain did. That cuckoo mind, dumping his thoughts from their nest and taking up residence with its own malefic designs and plots. It was like Russian roulette with vicious madness as the bullet in the gun.

The sun going down was a silent alarm, one that felt like an ice pick stabbing between its closed eyes. It stayed in the bag on the floor between the sofa and the coffee table and groaned. The pain between its eyes grew sharper, jabbed deeper. It felt its boxers grow wet as its bladder let go. It fumbled with numb fingers and found the zipper to escape. It pulled it down and rolled free of the quilted envelope it'd been sleeping in. A heady reek of sweat and fresh piss followed, almost indiscernible from the other odors in the dwelling. It stood and pulled down the urine-soaked boxers, stepped out of them and walked naked down the hall. The bathroom door slammed, and the silence held an anxious breath until it opened again.

The thing shambled back to the unkempt living room. It paused to kick the pissy shorts into the corner by the chair where the dead man sat. The Mouth walked by on its way into the kitchen, rubbing the corpse's shirtless distended belly like it was a Buddha. A high-pitched fart followed by a low gurgling noise came from somewhere under and the cushion of the chair grew darker. An orgy of flies took flight but didn't go far. The dead man's face still held an expression of surprise.

The Mouth remained blank faced as it turned on the faucet and let the water run while it picked up a pair of jeans from the pile in front of the washing machine. They were not clean, but it put them on anyway. It remained shirtless as it leaned forward to slurp hot water from the faucet. Wisps of steam rose from the sink as the hot water swirled the drain and glugged into oblivion. The plastic covered window above the sink fogged in the spots where the old trash bag had faded and grown brittle. The thing slurped and gulped loudly, as the hot water turned its cheeks and chin bright red. Still, it drank.

The Mouth was always parched.

10

———

Elijah read the note taped to the top of the plastic container in his hands. He was too old for notes from his mother, for instructions to things he'd been doing forever. He was too old for the little hearts at the bottom, but he would never put voice to such a thing.

He knew about time. He knew it was all we really have. Time is the only real constant. One day, he'd be sitting somewhere, eyes puffy and sore and he'd be looking at a picture of his weary mother and wishing more than anything that he could go get a dish from the fridge with a little note on the lid that said, "I love you," with a little heart after.

He removed the piece of paper and put it in his pocket. He'd put it in the box with the others when he got to his room. He put the noodles in the microwave and listened to its drone as it heated his meal from the inside out. He took that time to go into the living room and turn on the lamps, all three of them. He then ran upstairs and turned on the light in his room and in the bathroom. The door to his mother's room was closed and he left it that way. He could watch hours of horror films with monsters and maniacs and laugh the entire time, but when he was alone, when the sky bruised and the sun winked out, the darkness wouldn't do. His imagination would race and holler until he killed the darkness in 60-watt bursts.

Elijah scurried back down in time to hear the oven ding that his food was ready, took it out, and sprinkled black pepper on it. He grabbed a fork from the drainer by the sink and went into the other room.

Elijah sat in his mom's recliner to eat but not before he used a foot to punch the ON button on the TV. It was an old floor model, but it still worked fine. He sucked a cheesy string of pasta into his mouth as the opening music to the local evening news played. "Oh man," he sighed through the top story about some politician and a hooker, not really wanting to watch any of the program at all, but the channel changer was out of reach.

He forgot all about his disinterest when the banner at the bottom read *Another victim in Cordry*. He paused in mid-noodle slurp and leaned forward to hear better.

No name. No photo. Just that another person, this time a young woman, had been found viciously murdered. Her body had been discovered by a fisherman who had been making his way through the copse of trees to the creek early that morning. The man gave his name, Jamie, to the dude holding the microphone in his face. He looked shaken as he recounted how he was nearly to the water when he noticed something brightly colored in the weeds by the stony bank near the dam. He walked closer and saw the hot pink fabric of the girl's sweatshirt. He started to relay more, but they cut back to the studio. The news lady with the enormous hair said this brought the total of victims in this unsolved and ongoing story to three.

"Three? Three! What the hell?"

Elijah sat the bowl on the side table and ran to the back door, turned the knob lock, and set the deadbolt. He did the same for the front door before he returned to his perch in his mother's chair.

Dinner had been forgotten as he tried to figure out how a spate of murders in his fly speck town had escaped his radar for nearly two weeks. He hadn't even overheard gossip at the geezer home. He showered in record time, while visions of *Psycho* danced in his head. Within minutes he was back downstairs in the well-lit living room watching music videos, the biggest butcher knife from the drawer on the table beside him.

It was after ten o'clock when he surrendered to sleep, dozing off in the comfy chair, under one of his mother's afghans. A light on in every room and a big knife less than ten inches away.

"Elijah?"

His mother's voice held volume, but she had not yelled. He opened his sleepy eyes and deciphered his surroundings. The TV was still on, as were the lamps in the room and the ceiling light in the adjoining dining room and the one at the top of the stairs. He sighed and rubbed his eyes, stopping mid yawn when he remembered the butcher knife.

"I'm waiting. Why is every light in this damn house on? I don't work two jobs just to pay the electric bill, buddy."

She had fuzzies in her permed hair. Little puffs of light blue and yellow. She must have been working third shift at the sewing plant. Elijah couldn't keep her routine straight. The factory was her full-time gig, and she did a few shifts at the Pour House tending bar. Neither position glamorous, but they kept the bills paid and her body achingly tired.

"Is that my carving knife? What the hell?"

"I'm sorry, Mom. I was kinda scared after I saw the news last night. About the killings."

Her expression softened then, a bit, and she walked over

to where her son was. She knelt in front of the chair and wrapped him in her arms. He allowed it. And when she started to cry, he did his best not to sigh.

"Oh my God, Honey. I'm sorry. I hadn't even thought to tell you about that. You're such a good kid. You don't stray or wander so I wasn't as worried...as I guess I should have been. I didn't know there had been another one." She shook her head and one of the fuzzies dislodged and floated across the room on a phantom current of air. He thought of Horton and Whoville. Then he found himself wondering if the Whos in that story were the same ones the Grinch terror- ized. His brain was ridiculous.

"You know I don't chatter at work much. Those bitches are too catty for me. I just work. Eat my lunch in the car and then go finish my work. I guess if I'd paid attention, I'd have caught the gossip."

"It's okay, Mom. I just got nervous and didn't want to be where I couldn't run away easier. I've watched enough horror movies to know what to and not to do."

"That you have." She smiled but it was a weak thing. She stood and the sound of her knees popping could be heard over the volume of the television.

"I'm going to shower and hit the hay. Elijah, I don't care if you go across to visit Ken and Tierny today but nowhere else, please. Just here or there."

"Okay, Mom." His voice met the back of her as she slowly made her way up the stairs.

"The lights are all on up here too. Kiddo, if I made enough that you got an allowance, I'd garnish it for the damn light bill." She laughed after so he knew she wasn't mad. The woman was rarely mad at him. He was quite lucky.

12

The Mouth sat in the trailer. Hunkered down over the low toilet. Its stomach groaned and squealed like a prized hog. It bared its teeth, and its muscles inside rolled and flexed. Bones creaked. Splashing water warned seconds before the stench. The small room filled with the wretched smell; a low tide fish funk mixed with hot metal. Sharp enough to overpower the reek of the dead woman in the bathtub. The thing panted and stared at the floor between its feet, at the pill bottles that clotted the corner next to the tub where the trash can overflowed.

Its eyes zeroed in on the thick yellowing curls of its toenails. It clenched and unclenched its hands into fists, the tips of its overlong fingernails caked with dark matter and leaving creases in the calloused flesh of its palms.

The thing sat for several more minutes before it stood. It looked at the roll hanging on the hook beside him. The empty cardboard tube caused a boil of anger in its guts It growled like an animal and pulled a stiff towel from the shower curtain rod. It reeked of mildew and sweat. The thing dragged it over its backside and stared at the deep red mess it came away with. Things were wriggling there. It recalled the time it stomped on a hatchling when it was a kid. The remains that had been mashed into the stones behind the shed were gruesome. It held the towel in front of its chest and inhaled deeply. His eyes glossed over, and his stomach rumbled. It dropped the towel into the tub with the dead woman, almost obscuring the pale dimpled flesh and staring eyes.

The Mouth walked into the hall, where the shadows swallowed it, welcoming it as family.

13

Tierny was just getting out of his car when Elijah wolf-whistled at him from across the road. The bearded man cocked an arm and struck a ridiculous pin up pose, pursing lips in a kissy face. The boy laughed as he jogged across the two lanes. Tierny waited at the edge of the small lot until Elijah got there.

"Morning, Kiddo."

"Hi, Tier. How are you today?"

"Oh. I'm here. Still, I walk, still, I breathe. Has to be enough, yeah?"

"I suppose. Have you heard about the newest murder? I only saw it last night on the news. Had me all kinds of paranoid. I slept in the recliner by the door with a knife by my side. Ma was not pleased." He looked at his friend and smiled. Tierny threw one back, but it held no warmth, just a current of unease.

"Yeah. I've been following it a little. Scary shit. I didn't mention it to you or anyone here. These poor folks have enough to worry about."

Elijah lifted his satchel and patted its bulk. "I brought

some old movies to watch with Ken today in the rec room, if Vera isn't hogging the TV with her damn soaps. She sleeps through half of them anyway."

"C'mon, I love Vera. But she won't be in the big room. She's resting today."

Elijah could tell by Tierny's voice, he was keeping something back, so he called him on it.

"What's happened to her?" The boy could look years older when the need arose. Tierny looked at him and breathed out through his nose. It whistled.

"She had a small stroke yesterday afternoon. Then a second one last night. She's ok as of now but needs to rest until we see what the after effects will be. She already didn't get around too well. And well...she's old."

"Yeah. I'm sorry, Tier." Elijah patted Tierny's arm and the bigger man put his hand over the boy's and squeezed it once, quickly.

"Thank you. Now, let me get to work and you go get that old man moving. What movies are you watching?"

"I brought *The Mummy's Hand* and *Reptilicus*."

"Jesus, that's a pair. If I get a free minute or ten, I'll slip in. I love *Reptilicus*. I saw it on the weekend horror theater show when I was a kid."

"Ok. Have a good day, Tier."

Tierny nodded and flicked his cigarette butt to the ground. He walked to the side door and was inside before Elijah had cleared the lot.

The boy walked slowly, thinking about Tierny. The man was so much fun, but he could tell the job nibbled at him, sometimes going for a full chomp. His kind heart was a sore that the fingers of the home couldn't leave be, working at the edges of any scab that threatened to form. He worked in a constant state of inflammation he could easily jettison for an easier job. But he felt he owed the old people this. They toiled for decades to pave the way for the younger folks, often to be forgotten or tossed aside and scorned, Tierny was a beacon for them. They knew it and he could see that Tier basked in the glow they gave back.

But when the glow faded and eventually burned out completely, it wrecked him. Every single time.

Elijah opened the door and ducked inside as the first raindrops hit the ground.

14

Ken sat in the chair by the window, while he watched the first of the movies the boy brought. He half-listened to the drumming of the rain on the ground outside. The blinds were drawn and the room dim.

Elijah knelt at the television and ejected the mummy movie. He held up the box for *Reptilicus* and smiled at the old man. It was too dim for him to make out what the movie was, and he could not recall what the boy had said. Ken nodded but held up a lone finger.

"Perhaps, we will take a break. I need to walk a little. My knees are about to send letters of forlorn recollection to my feet." He chuckled at himself, and Elijah dropped the movie to the carpet and went to him, helping him out of the chair.

The man was a bit unsteady today. His feet seemed unsure of the ground beneath them. His whole body was practically vibrating. Elijah held his arm and helped aid him to the hall. He stood by the desk and watched Holly filling in the log sheets. She looked up at them and smiled, but it was her *I'm busy, you two, go find something to get into, please.* The boy nodded and he and Ken went back to the room they had just left. He walked them to the table by the window and eased Ken down into the chair.

"I'll go see if I can get Mary in the kitchen to give us some snacks."

"Just for you, boy. I'm fine. I'm still full from the sandwich you brought me. I'm just a bit tired today. Sleep has been a bitch to catch the past few nights."

"I don't sleep well a lot of the time either. My brain is noisy. Last night, I slept in Mom's chair after I watched the news. I was afraid to go upstairs. There's been some unsolved murders in and around Cordry and it gave me the nerves. Ma calls it the heebeegeebees."

"Death has a way of fraying nerves. I've not heard about these deaths. I'll have to get a paper."

"Three, so far. A woman, a young dude, and a girl. The most recent one, that girl, was like sixteen. The fella was, I think, twenty-five and the first lady was in her fifties. They all had their throats cut or torn out, I think that's what the news chick said, that blonde with the poofy hair."

Ken nodded and stared at the floor as though it were water, and he was stranded by it. He kept his eyes on the thick yellow shag and after a long five minutes, began to speak.

"Elijah, go to my room and get in the drawer of my night table. There's money there. Take some and pop over to the Kwik-Sell and get me all the local papers and hurry right back."

"Ma told me not to go anywhere but here. But I guess it's just the end of the street. Okay."

"Good boy. Take enough to buy yourself a soda. Not root beer though. I can't bear to hear you belching all afternoon. Sounding like a bear." The old man rolled his eyes and the kid laughed. He scurried off down the hall to get the money.

Ken reached out for the cord that hung from the blinds. He pulled until they rose enough for him to see out into the side yard of the facility. He scanned the tree line and saw that the rain had stopped. Everything had that soaked and drab look. He noted a few bright birds flitting around the berry bushes near the edge of the woods, and almost missed the man. Ken pursed his lips and squinted through the strip of space between the blind and window ledge.

The man was slight, almost gaunt. He stood with his hands in his pockets and even from a distance he looked dirty. His shirt, wrinkled and baggy, hung on him like a shroud. Jeans that were frayed at the cuffs and hung loose and bunchy the way denim that hasn't been laundered in a while gets.

Ken leaned forward, his nose almost touching the cold glass. The man had no shoes and his face was thin. Very thin. He had a scraggle of stubble covering his cheeks, but the sharp structure of his bones could be seen. He just stood and looked at the building. Ken felt the hairs on his neck dance. Ants marched along his spine. He swallowed hard.

"I took the ten you had. I'll bring your change right back." Elijah stood just inside the doorway.

"Hold on, son. Let's watch that other movie first. It's started raining out there again." Ken lied with an ease born of a long lifetime, no trace of the nervousness that was snarling his guts. Elijah paused and then nodded and went to the set and put the video in.

15

"That was awful, Elijah."

"Oh, I know, but it's pretty fun. That monster?" The kid laughed and it was a sweet sound that the room absorbed like a dry sponge. Places like that, devoid of joy mostly, sucked up the splinters and shards of happiness that sometimes appeared like a great black leech.

The boy slid the tape from the mouth of the VCR and back into the cardboard sleeve, which he carried to the small couch along the side of the room and put into his canvas bag. Ken leaned closer to the window, peering like a nosey neighbor.

"Anything exciting out there?"

The old man said nothing. His lips disappeared and his eyes were almost closed.

"Well, I'll go for your papers now. I'll be right back."

Ken stared at the spot where the strange man had been ninety minutes earlier. The spot between the large white tree and the trio of squat berry bushes. He saw the spots of red and brown on the mulchy soil where the odd man's feet had stood. He made a snicking noise with his tongue upon the realization they were the corpses of the birds. A cardinal and a couple of robins. The gray sky parted like a grand curtain and fingers of sunlight fell through. The birds smoldered and were gone within minutes.

Elijah stared at his friend, slightly annoyed but patient. "I'm going." He spoke louder. This time Ken heard him and looked to where the boy hovered in the entryway.

"Okay. Quick as a flash and be careful."

Elijah left and the old man made himself look away from the window. He stared at the carpet and tried to sift through the sandy wreckage of his memories for the reason why the man seemed so oddly familiar.

16

E lijah hunkered down by the long wooden shelf that held the newspapers and magazines. He had Ken's papers on the floor by his foot while he perused the new issue of *Fangoria*. Not typical small town convenience store fodder, but Steve Scott, the owner, liked Elijah and had gone to school with his mom, so he made sure to get it in.

" 'Li, I get that in just for you so you can buy it, you know."

"I know, Mr. Scott. Thanks. But I have to wait until the weekend when I get my money from Mrs. Shell for cutting her grass the other day."

"Okay. But save some for then. Deal?" The man laughed and turned his attention back to the fellow buying Pall Malls and a bottle of ginger ale.

Elijah stood and carried the papers to the cooler where he got a bottle of Squirt for himself. He took it all to the counter and handed the ten to Steve.

"I thought you were broke, pal? And we're into the current events now, are we?"

"These are for Ken at the old folk's home. He wants to read about the murders."

The smile Steve had been wearing slipped into something like a frown, but sadder.

"That's bad business. Truly terrible."

"I saw about them on the news, that big haired lady said they had their throats cut."

"That's not all." The man looked around to make sure no one else was within earshot and leaned down to be face to face with the boy.

"I'm only telling you this because I know you can stomach it. I heard this from Marty over at the funeral parlor, how I know it to be true. They had their throats *ripped* out, not exactly cut. There was almost no blood left in the bodies, but more than that. Weirder than that. Most of the veins, arteries were gone too. Nothing... anything that has to do with a body's blood at all, just gone."

Steve stopped speaking when the bell sounded, and the door opened as old Harriet Forney hobbled in with her cane. He smiled as she waddled back to the cooler that held the milk and eggs.

"Is that true? I mean, what is that about? I know I've read that some killers keep stuff, like mementos but how does one keep a circulatory system?" Elijah said, incredulous.

"Scout's honor, that's what Marty told me." Steve held up a hand and made a solemn face. Elijah just held out his hand for the change.

The boy had a look of surprise and perhaps a sprinkle of excitement, as he left the store. He waved at Steve before the door swished closed behind him, and the cowbell clanged where it was tied to the door handle.

17

It was nearly five o' clock. The day was starting to roll itself up to make way for dusk. The Mouth sat in the corner of the living room, in the darkened little cave he had made for himself by pulling the sofa against the wall at an angle. He had thrown all the blankets and sheets he had over it, making something like a fort that a child would make.

In its belly, he sat naked. His skin was pink and puffy from his foray into the daylight. Even overcast sunshine licked him raw. Tiny points of white speckled him and wept sticky moisture. The largest concentration of them covered his chest and abdomen. He stared into the air as the flickering of the small candle on the floor danced in the small space. Three jars of dark red were stacked like blocks along the base of the wall. Things sloshed and moved in them. Swam in the ruby slurry. He paid them no mind. His head was filled with the song and voices of celebration. The thing he had been seeking for so very long had been found.

For seemingly endless years, he had wandered the earth and swallowed time and space as a feast. He had been Jonah in the stomach of the whale. He had been the hammer in the Roman soldier's hand. He had heard it kissing the nail through the savior's palm. He was the bullet that had felled countless men. He was the hollow thing they died for. He was the hole in their heads that drooled brains and blood. He had swirled the drain of the world for so many years, times so many more. He was the mouth that never filled. The mouth that never chewed and never spoke. The mouth that swallowed and swallowed and swallowed. Black promise behind gray teeth.

He was The Mouth.

18

B efore he was The Mouth, Randall Horst was a recluse.

He lived mostly by wits and patience in the forest on the eastern border of Ohio. He had built the shack with his own bare hands, so deep in the woods that even when the weather grew cold and he fired his stove, no one saw or cared. He was a bother to no one. He hiked and foraged for berries and morels, trapped, and hunted for meat when he had no money to buy. He lived mostly off the grid and that was how he liked it.

His small, rustic dwelling was decorated with rusted tin signs and moldering pin-up girl centerfolds. Long shelves were crammed with treasures found during hikes in the woods, and dozens of bottles varying in size, shape, and color. Crocks and jugs. Musket balls and old bullets. A few knife blades and stone ax heads. It was a museum, a shrine to time untouched under the shade of tall trees with long thick arms.

The last treasure he remembered finding, before his sanity took leave, was tangled in the branches of a very old oak near the base of the mountain. It was probably still laying on the table in the shack he abandoned: a small, pale green bottle. What was once thick twine, withered by age to thin string, tied in a stubborn knot, the other end, tied to a faded piece of thin rubber. The remnants of a balloon. The tarnished metal cap, most likely still on the floor where he dropped it. So surprised was he, when he opened it and what was inside came out.

In fleeting moments, when The Mouth was resting or busy arguing with the other voices that live within, and as all the dark shapes and red ringed mouths chitter and din in the confines of his skull, a very small child of shadow stands to the back. When he steps to the light, his cherubic face is split and fuming. When the whispers scurry from the ruin of his mouth, that is when the others mumble harder-louder-crushing the shadow boy's pleas under the weight of their cacophony.

Randall would swim up through the inky mire that held him and nearly break the surface, would try to think and to remember for a feeble moment before being found out, and then he would feel the many hands grasping his ankles to pull him back down. They remind Randall that he is a vehicle, like a mother's womb or a little green bottle. That he is theirs. That *he* is gone. When the legion tells him this, the shadow boy to the back nods and keeps nodding.

19

The sun peeked over the mountain, a luminous Kilroy. Tierny sat in his truck, book in front of his bearded face. The window was halfway down, and a plume of smoke floated lazily from it. He clamped the butt of his cigarette between his lips as he turned the page. The radio was on, but the volume was low, the Go-Go's just barely audible.

"Hey Tier!" Elijah yelled as he popped up from beneath the driver's side window, where he had stealthily crept. Tierny jumped and the cigarette fell from his mouth into his lap. The man squirmed as he brushed himself to make sure his smoke was on the floor. He opened the door and hopped out. Spying the smoldering filter on the floor, he squashed it under his sneaker. He turned and gave the boy a scowl.

"Why the hell would you do that?" He was breathing a bit harder than usual. His face was red, and he was not smiling. Not like Tierny at all.

"I thought it would be funny. I guess it wasn't, I'm sorry."

"It's okay. But man, you nearly gave me a heart attack. I was just reading on my lunch and in my own world."

"What're you reading? Not Ken's book again?"

"Heh. No." Tierny leaned into the vehicle and grabbed the book where it had been flung, caught in the space between the passenger seat and the door. He showed Elijah the cover and smiled. *The Real History of Vampires: Written in Red.*

"Wow. That looks like some shit. You reading that because of the murders?"

"I mean, yeah, but not really. I read this kinda shit all the time. And yeah, there is a lot of bunk in here, for sure, but there are still some fairly intriguing ideas. There's a story in here about a fellow who had a parasitic twin that he essentially absorbed in the womb. He carried out horrible deeds and when he was put down and autopsied, they found teeth and hair in his brain. The claim was that his brother had committed the crimes, had basically taken the wheel, and driven his able brother to do it. Lots of wild, wild shit and theories. Like the thought that vampires are actually based on ancient cases of symbiotic personality maladies, sort of like split personalities but in a weirder way. Almost like possession."

"Go on. But first, you have ashes in your beard." Elijah hopped up on the tailgate of the small truck, it was broken and always hung open. Tierny raked his fingers through the coarse hair and wiped them on his jeans.

"Like, say a guy had this affliction. Or condition. Whatever. He'd be himself and then the other personality would slide into the driver's seat occasionally. Drive him to act on usually irrational impulses. That part would be in charge for who knew how long before it abandoned the controls to the full-time personality...who had no inkling that anything had transpired. So, they'd find the signs and clues of the atrocities committed by the other self and they would often help in trying to find the culprit, unaware it was them."

"Like, a good man, until the other personality took over, and then maybe he killed kids or something? That's some Jekyll and Hyde shit. Creepy."

"It is, but it makes sense. Strip that vampire stuff away, I mean, and I'm sure this concept has influenced many of the horror tropes we see. We could have a decent person who is essentially kidnapped and blindfolded while their other self runs amok. Then when they're done, they yank the bag from the good self's head and let them deal with the carnage. Maybe literally."

"What if it's more like a seeing eye dog?"

"Go on." Tierny was smiling. He loved it when they spit-balled crackpot, darkly themed pontifications like they were playing ping pong.

"Like a fella who can't see but the dog is his eyes. What if a fella was just a normal fella but part of his secret self was dark or broken or something. And instead of having a dog to see for him that everyone else could see...what if the other personality was something like that? But invisible. Like an armless dude and a dude with hands would make a perfect pair."

"Dude. That's pretty good. A bit cumbersome but I think the basic points are sound. Like the person is a vampire. But the person is right as rain until they're possessed by the monster sense–the mouth or teeth are like symptoms and then they're the monster until that phantom sense leaves them. Like what if those enhanced monstrous senses are standalone entities. What if a vampire is a colony creature like coral?"

Tierny held out the palm of his hand and Elijah slapped

it with his own. The smack echoed across the small parking lot.

"Okay, 'Li. I have to go back to work. Are you going to see Ken?"

"I was going to check on him. I dropped by yesterday and all he did was read those newspapers and he looked so tired."

"Yeah. He isn't sleeping well. I've seen that before with dementia folks. Early on, they realize that thoughts are missing. Things they always knew or did...and they rationalize it as theft of a sort, and they don't let themselves sleep so they can keep guard. Protect themselves, so to speak."

"That's sad." Elijah held the door open, and the bearded man went ahead. The boy followed and let the door slam closed.

"Well, Kiddo. I'm off to divvy pills and help get lunch trayed. I'll see you when I get to Ken's room."

"Okay, Tier. Have fun. And don't put any Jello on Ken's tray. He won't eat it anyway."

"I think it's vanilla pudding today."

"Bring that. If he doesn't eat it, I will."

"I can bring you your own," Tierny made a stern face. "Stealing an old man's pudding."

They laughed as they went their different directions. Holly sat at the nurse's station, filling out papers, and did not pay either of them any mind.

20

J eff Prettyman had finished taking in the last stack of newspapers when he heard the jingling of the strap of bells nailed to the door. He paused for a moment to see if it was just due to the door slowly closing. The hinges were sometimes stiff on damp days. He thought he heard the scuff of feet on the wooden floor.

"Be right there," he shouted from where he was hunkered behind the counter, fighting to cut through the plastic band with his dull pocketknife. "We aren't quite open yet, but if you hold tight a minute, I'll sort you." His tongue popped out of the corner of his mouth while he sawed the band with the small blade.

If I didn't want them open, the damn band would've snapped while I carried them in and they'd have fallen all over the sidewalk.

The band snapped with a loud pop and Prettyman laid his knife on the counter while he grabbed the edge to steady himself as he stood. His nostrils flared at the stench that filled the front of the store. Sour and fermented. It reminded him of his house visits when he delivered medication to diabetics. There was a smell. Not down to hygiene really, just the weird way their body was betraying them. He scanned the four aisles that ran the length from the counter and saw there was no one.

"Hello?" his voice nearly echoed in the empty store. He saw the pharmacy counter at the back end, still shrouded in shadow. He didn't open that until around ten or whenever Jenn decided to come in to take over the front counter. Small towns didn't run on a stopwatch. He walked out, around and down the second aisle. His footsteps seemed to boom in the quiet. He stopped and stood still for long minutes until he decided he was alone.

The bell must have just been a breeze before the door had fully swung closed. He rubbed the back of his neck with his left hand and mumbled to himself as he rounded the corner. He was about to unlock the safe and grab the morning's till when the shadow fell upon him. He looked up into the face of the one who had made it.

His mouth opened and closed like a fish out of water, his eyes bugged out and wide. The man before him was tall and seemed to grow as he watched, stretching over him. His dirty T-shirt shortened as his torso lengthened. His arms stayed at his sides and Prettyman noted that his pocketknife was in the man's right hand. Something wet hit his cheek and Prettyman looked up into the intruder's face. The mouth was spread wide and crammed with teeth like awl points. Prettyman's brain was hollering, even as his mouth failed him.

Please God, let someone come in for something. Please!

The stranger's empty hand landed on Prettyman's shoulder, pinning him in place. The weight of the force the man used to push down made Prettyman's knees pop. Flames of discomfort sprinted up his legs. Still, the strange man pushed down while Prettyman fought to remain upright.

"Help." He croaked and it was a small thing in a large space. Lost immediately.

"No one is coming." The intruder spoke flatly, but his mouth had not moved, his teeth glistening with drool. The voice was in Prettyman's head as though someone were whispering in his ear.

Prettyman opened his mouth to shout for help, but his knees hit the floor before he could follow through. The hand kept pushing down on him with ridiculous force. Prettyman's kneecaps ground into the hardwood until the left one split. The yowl he unleashed was a great thing that flew to the corners of the ceiling above. He went blind with agony but willed himself to survey the damage, regardless of the fact there was a monster in his space. He saw the cloth of his trousers pulled taut by the instantaneous swelling of his knees, over-risen dough craving a slice or pinch to alleviate the pressure.

The strange man-thing leaned forward and put its mouth over Prettyman's. The old man released his scream, swallowed by the monster along with his tongue. The creature sucked with such force that Prettyman felt it in his chest as his lungs were pulled. His throat grew warm, and he could taste the rising blood. His vision grew weak, and he noted the frosted front window was marred by the silhouettes of passersby but not one came into the shop. Not one caused the bells to ring. Something tore in his chest and in the mad seconds before his eyes closed, he watched as it slid down the monster's throat with a noticeable bulge. It was like a snake swallowing a rabbit. The shop quieted save for the wet sounds of sucking.

Jeff Prettyman was left on the floor of the store that had

been his father's, and his father's father's before that. His eyes stared at the old, tin ceiling. His body cooled. The Mouth was an efficient beast. Not a drop of blood anywhere. His pocketknife was back on the counter, where he had put it.

Several flies had found him and camped out on his open eyes by the time the bells rang, and Ethel Madron waddled in for her Epsom salts. Her screams were heard the next block over.

21

"You heard about Prettyman?" Elijah half whispered.

He looked up as Rose came out from the back with his pizza slice and their drinks. Tierny thanked her and Elijah nodded. Tierny looked at Elijah across the table. At this time of day, the pizza shop was practically empty. Tierny cleared his throat to test how their voices might carry. He grabbed his smokes from his flannel pocket before he remembered he couldn't smoke there and pulled his fingers back as though there were a rat trap in the pocket.

"I did. I stopped by Scott's this morning for smokes, and he told me. Said they think he musta fell. He was on the counter for some reason and jumped down and his knees broke, and he fell and broke something inside...bled out."

"How could that happen and there also be almost no blood like the others? I mean, how is that even a thing? That counter is maybe four feet high if that. It might hurt but would it snap your legs?" Elijah mumbled while from his mouth, a stringer of cheesy hung from his lips to the triangle in his hand.

"He had cancer. Some weird bone kind of shit. They were brittle. That's what Steve said Marty told him. So, he jumped down and the force broke his knees, and he fell, and more bones broke and punctured organs, and he bled to death." Tierny looked to see where Rose the waitress was, and saw they were alone in the room. He could hear her and Sebastian arguing in the kitchen, all but the profanity in Italian.

He leaned in closer. "Except there was no blood at all. And his lips were all shredded and full of holes like he'd eaten a barbed wire sandwich."

"Well, now we know one thing that could tie this to the killer."

"I was thinking the very same, I think it highly unlikely that we'd have a separate killer working in this turd of a town at the same time."

"We gotta figure out who it is. The town isn't that fucking big. We can't wait for the cops to do it."

"Language, little man. I let you slide with the damns, hells, and shits, but I turn a blind eye to the F bomb, and you get cocky at home, let it slip, I don't want any blame if your Ma stops letting you bum around with us anymore. She's already not keen on us hanging out all the time." He drank from his cup of soda and wiped his lips.

Elijah nodded as he shoveled the rest of his slice into his mouth.

"What was the second thing?" Tierny drained his cup and rattled the ice cubes for no reason other than emphasis.

"Oh, that ol' Steve Scott is not the person to tell a secret to. Dude spills all the beans."

"Definitely true. But can you blame him? A small town

like this? Time has teeth and gnaws slowly. You'd go nuts if you had nothing to do, and gossip is a valid pastime to some."

"I think we could figure it out. We're smart and we know about monsters. And we can get Ken to help us. For sure before the local police get a handle. Hell, this town isn't even big enough for its own real cop. We have one that we share with like four other small towns within fifteen miles, any direction. They'll never crack it."

"Jesus, old Ken would be like having our own Jessica Fletcher, if she was a cranky old man with early dementia instead, or if Paul McCartney was an Avon lady."

"He's smart as f—as hell." Elijah countered, completely not getting the joke Tierny just made.

"He is." Tierny shook his head, sad that he'd wasted a good one liner on a kid who was too young to get it. He stood and laid a folded five on the table and nodded to the boy. "Pay with that and meet me outside. I need to smoke while I think."

"Okie doke." Elijah finished chewing the crust and washed it down with his root beer. His burps were going to annoy Ken, and thinking about it made him smile.

22

Ken sat in the wheelchair in the big room. The television was on, the volume turned up because Peter had turned it on, and he was deaf as a post. Ken paid him and the TV set no mind, as he stared out the window. The trees took small bows in the winds that blew across the neighboring field and the home's wide yard. Ken's mind was elsewhere.

'One ought to not have to bury their child. A mother should die before those she bore.' Ava's eyes are red, wild things hiding in her skull, prowling behind them. She is so drawn and thin. She has not been eating, not in the weeks since Brian passed. Ken just sits at the table and nurses his coffee. She sits on her side and weeps into the handkerchief in her hand. The sounds are soft but forceful. Ken does not meet her eyes. Cannot. He has so many secrets, he's practically made of them. Now would not be the time to tell any of them to try and ease her pain. Brown liquid scalds his pursed lips and he not only allows it, he welcomes it. A new burn to help forget the others.

Try being practically immortal. Any idea what it is like watching all your family die and then searching, then finding, then building another only to have it happen again? A bombshell like that would not help. She'd think him mad and how wrong would she be? A lifetime can drive anyone off the rails a little, but living several in your one? If he were of a mind, he could tell her he has outlived seven of his own children and three other wives before her. He could tell her he buried his parents before her own grandmother had been born, while her grandmother's grand- mother was a child. Time waits for no man, but me. For me, the bastard lingers and dawdles and thumbs his nose at every provocation.

My God.

He looks down at the hand that holds the crockery mug, at the band of silver around his finger. He winces as the hot, bitter liquid meets his lips and allows his gaze to settle on his wife with her crying. He knows he will bury her as well. He swallows and decides this is it. He will not wed again. His heart is a mansion so full of ghosts, he has no more room. So many memories shrouded beneath dusty sheets. So many stilled voices that whisper to him in his sleep. He puts down the mug and sits there silent until her weeping ceases. It seems like a lifetime.

He is pulled from the tar pit of his memories by laughter in the hall. The high-pitched giggling comes from the boy. The throatier laugh from Tierny. Ken draws in a deep breath and smooths his hair down and fastens on his best fake smile. In his weary head, he is thinking about the respite that will come from forgetting it all.

23

"I have been reading these papers. The articles on these poor souls, while as simply written as they are, they do provide the basic details. It's as good a foundation as any." Ken licks his lips and leans back in the chair. He looks around the rec room and the three of them are its only inhabitants. Tierny sat down at the table and occupied his fidgeting fingers with a small sliver of the plastic trim on its edge. Elijah, on the floor, cross-legged with a notebook open on one knee, pen in hand.

"So, let's start with a list of facts. I'll just write it all down since I doubt Paula or Holly will let us tape pictures and notecards to the wall and use tacks and thread like they do on the cop shows." Elijah smiled when he said it, but Ken's look remained stern.

"No jokes here, boy. Death, those of this manner, removes the levity. Well, death is stony of face, always. I've known him a long, long time and the man is all dark business."

Elijah and Tierny shared a look, one with raised

eyebrows and a slight tilt of the head towards Ken, who did not notice.

"Sorry." Elijah said, "I'll print so anyone can read it. My cursive is awful."

'Everyone's cursive is awful." Tierny remarked.

Ken paid them no attention as he opened the first newspaper from the small pile in his lap. Touched his thumb to his tongue and turned another page, repeated the act.

"Here. The first one was the older woman. Found in her own yard. In her own garden. Her throat cleanly opened and barely a drop of blood on the ground or her body. That blood business isn't in the paper, the young mister here gave me that second hand from the convenience store fellow."

"Steve Scott."

"Yes, him. Then less than a week later, we have victim number two. A young man, early

twenties. He was found in his driveway, half under his own vehicle. His neck was not as cleanly opened but again, not much blood left in or around him."

The old man paused while the boy wrote the notes in his neat print.

"Go on." Elijah said after he wrote the last of the note on the second victim.

"The third victim, the poor girl, was found by a fisherman near the creek. Close to the dam, I believe. Same method of dispatch and the only real difference being the fact the body was found a good distance from her home. The other two were on their own doorsteps, practically."

"And poor Mr. Prettyman. He was killed in his shop. Broad daylight." Tierny said.

"Ah, yes. And he had extra damage other than the mouth and throat damage as the others, his knees were broken, I believe." Ken nodded to Elijah for affirmation and the boy gave it in a returned nod. Ken's brow furrowed and he held up an arthritic finger. "You said that Prettyman was killed in broad daylight. We have no way of knowing when the others met their demise. Day time or nighttime. Think this is of import?"

The newsprint crinkled loudly as Ken folded it and dropped the pile onto the floor beside his chair. In the light from the window, he looked his claimed age, like he could actually be almost two hundred and fifty years old. His skin was a landscape of small wrinkles, in soft light or a dim room, he looked like anyone's grandfather. In this moment in the kiss of sunshine, he appeared ancient. The boy was still writing, and Tierny was staring at the floor, obviously thinking.

Ken cleared his throat. "Thoughts. Ideas. Tierny, you go first."

Tierny started, then stood and smoothed his scrub shirt down over his slight paunch. He was about to speak when Ken shook his head.

"Sit down, boy. This isn't an AA meeting or a town rally. It's three friends kicking around ideas."

Tierny sat and leaned forward. "If I weren't a rational man, I'd be thinking vampires. My lifelong love of the spooky and scary makes that my go to, but..."

"Why a but? Why do you assume that cannot be the culprit?"

"'Cause they aren't real." Elijah tapped his pen on the edge of the notebook for emphasis.

"They aren't?" Ken arched an eyebrow and held it for a beat before he continued. "They do not exist, not in the sense you hapless bastards have been force fed by your spooky books and horror shows. They do not transform into bats or wolves. They do not fly or turn to mist. They can see their ugly selves in a mirror the same as anyone else. They don't fret for garlic or running water. If you throw a knotted string before them, they'd think you were mad. Only the snooty ones wear medallions and capes." The old man smiled.

"I had been wondering about that. The girl near the dam snagged my bloodsucker theory because of the proximity with the creek." Tierny drummed his fingers as he spoke, dying for a cigarette.

"The vampire of story and screen is, to put it crudely, bullshit. As with any stereotype, I suppose there are flecks of truth within, somewhere, but you'd be hard pressed to find them amongst the tripe." Ken's voice was getting sturdier, the more he spoke.

"So, Ken, what are real vampires then?"

Ken steepled his fingers and smiled down at the boy. "Tired and old, but mostly tired. And hungry."

"Do they drink blood to survive?" Elijah continued to write in the notebook.

The old man shook his head. "Not always. They require life, and life is up for interpretation. I feel that a true vampire craves—needs—that which has eluded it. Blood is often the screen and page stand in, as blood is a necessity for life. But can it also be love? Can someone denied any affection or sense of belonging be driven to devour it?" Ken's voice faded on the last words and there was a faraway look in his blue eyes. He was on the move, somewhere else.

Elijah opened his mouth but said nothing. Instead he looked to Tierny, who just shook his head in a subtle *no*. Silence settled upon the trio, but it seemed that all had fizzled out when Ken started to speak again, his voice a craggy falsetto, rusted and barbed. His eyes squinted in consternation.

"Hold the string. My pappy used to take me fishing in the dark. Tie a piece of chicken and drop it from the side of the boat. Hold the string and wait; don't let go or even let the length slip a little. Goes too deep and the bottomfeeders'll get it. Hold level and drag in the boat wake. You'll get a bite. Don't let it go. Think of that balloon string like that. Hold your brother safe in hand. Let go too soon and the bottom dwellers will come snapping for him, fixin' to hitch a ride on that poor little soul."

Ken's pale tongue snaked out to capture the frothy spittle from his chin. He sighed and his eyes opened fully, he coughed and looked at the man and boy before him. He frowned slightly as he hunched forward and resumed speaking, this time in his normal crepe paper voice.

"I let go of the balloon, you see. Grandmother told me to hold it tight. She said she would tell me when I could let it go. The right time was important, she said. Spine of night, she said, and shushed my mouth with her dirty finger. She held the candle. She held the bottle the string was tied to. I held the string to my brother. I looked up at the face of the moon. Ancient and bony. I stared at my small hand and just uncurled my fingers. I stood in the field and watched it go up and up and up. A shadow blur against the moon's white face. Behind me, grandmother howled in the night. Still, she howls."

Elijah noticed tears at the corners of the old man's eyes, and there was a tremble to his lips. Elijah looked to Tierny who nodded to the notebook and made a gesture with his hand like he was scribbling.

Write this ALL down. Every word.

The boy's pen began to move once again, and then it stopped. Something niggled at the back of the boy's brain. Something Ken had told him of his grandmother days ago. Elijah hoped pausing would cause the recollection to hitch and clarify its reason for lodging in his brain, but it didn't, so he resumed writing. Ken had fallen silent once more. He looked concerned and puzzled at the same time. Elijah looked to Tierny and then turned back to his old friend.

"Was it your birthday?" His young voice wavered in the big, empty room.

Ken looked down into the boy's bright eyes. There was little he recognized there now. He managed to smile and raised his index finger, pointed to the ceiling.

"I'm...no, I fear not, son. For me, it was quite the opposite. It was my... the nail in my palm, so to speak. It was the worst gift I ever received. I watched the balloon rise, heard Gramma wailing. She glared at me and said I would bear the brunt now. I had no idea what she meant, but the attention from her, oh, how I loved it."

The boy looked at Tierny, who again motioned for him to capture this all in his notes.

"Young man, could I go to my room? I'm very tired." Ken sounded weary and he seemed out of it, more than only slightly.

Tierny rose from the table and considered helping the old man from the chair, but decided to just wheel him. As Tierny turned the chair to face the door into the hall, Ken patted Elijah on the top of the head. Elijah looked up at the wizened face and watched him speak.

"My brother hides among the many. The shadows that scream and whisper. The darkness that crowds one's mind and heart. They kick the fuss, and my dear brother stands silent and waits. Bides his time."

"His time for what?" Elijah mumbles, standing up from his spot on the floor.

"Nice boy. He's such a good lad, yes?" Ken spoke mostly to Tierny.

"Yeah, he is. Let's get you to bed, Mr. Allenwood." Tierny said, hoping the use of his surname might be more recognizable to his fogged mind at that moment. As they got to the entrance, the bearded man turned and spoke to the boy, still standing with the notebook in his hands.

"I'll be back in a few minutes. Stay put."

Elijah nodded. He heard them in the hallway. He heard Ken once again mention the balloon and that someone was coming. And when he was sure they were gone, allowed himself to be saddened by what had just happened. How quickly the shift had occurred, how much it seemed as though his friend had quickly been replaced by a stranger. It must be even more jarring to the person experiencing it. In a blink, suddenly all faces seem foreign, all places too. Elijah felt weight settling on him as these realizations came to roost. He did not cry, but he felt a hot stinging in his chest. Another pin of adulthood in the voodoo doll of his heart.

24

"That was upsetting and odd." Elijah slid the last half of the vanilla wafer into his mouth and chewed.

"Upsetting, you ain't kidding. Odd, sadly, not at all. That's how dementia works. I mean, in that there are no set templates for anything. The person can be clear and present and within seconds, a curtain is yanked, a window is thrown open and a thick mist rolls in, but even in that fog they may sort of know who or where they are... or they may not. It's ghastly and heartbreaking."

The boy emptied his glass of milk and slid it towards the center of the table, next to the notebook.

"What was that balloon business, just like a crossed wire thought or something? He told me a story the other day, maybe last week. I had asked him for a personal detail. I wanted to *know* him better. See if he really believed he was an ancient vampire. He told me about the day he was born and how he was one of twins."

"His brother was named Vestus."

"His brother was born deformed and dead and his

grandmother was some sort of mountain witch, and from what I gathered from his story, she did something with Ken's dead brother, maybe a rite or something, and then disappeared. For years, he said. But he said just now that she had given him the balloon on his birthday."

"So, I think that's a legit link somehow. I mean, it seems like his mind had left the building, but there's glue there sticking it to facts, sorta."

"I have no idea. Maybe, but I doubt it. There's validity to everything he says. It's just that with his condition, sometimes... eventually constantly, it presents as a broken plate we need to put back together. Sometimes we have all the shards. Other times we don't. I feel like it wasn't entirely random, his balloon talk. It made sense to him. It tied in somehow. I told you to write it down because when he's clear again, maybe ask him and he can recall what he meant or why it was mentioned. But it's interesting that his brother was named Vestus and he named the main character in his book after him. Not a surprise, I mean most writers aren't really telling stories, they're shouting about themselves, their lives, and struggles. Doing it from behind the curtain so their voices don't dry up in terror of being heard."

They sat quiet for minutes. Tierny looked at the clock on the wall.

"It's like thrift store puzzles." Elijah spoke, but it was barely a whisper.

"What's that, Kiddo?" Tierny leaned forward and looked him in the eyes.

Elijah could tell Tierny was tired. The man's left eye was lazing just a little.

"That's how you first described Ken's dementia to me that day you were smoking out under the willow. You said his thoughts were going to be like buying a puzzle at the thrift store and putting it together and seeing that there were some pieces missing. You said we'd still get the gist of the big picture, but we'd have to fill in the blanks."

Tierny made his lips disappear and breathed out through his nose, making his mustache move. He slowly nodded and stood up from the table and spoke, his voice was poised to crack with emotion.

"I need to get back to work. It's almost time to get dinner prep ready. You go home. Or go find someone your own age to hang about with for a bit. You can't waste all your time with a weirdo introvert uncle-in-law and a doddering old man."

"Don't call him that. He can't help it."

"I'm sorry, I didn't mean it in a malicious way, just trying to joke a bit. But yeah, go find some kids to play with. You keep hanging around with us here and you'll never get laid."

They both laughed, but it was hollow.

"See you later, 'Li, probably tomorrow." Tierny said, and the man left the room and Elijah rose, grabbed the notes, and followed.

"See you tomorrow, Tier."

They went their opposite directions. The rec room held nothing but furniture, silence and shadows for hours after.

25

The Mouth had practically stopped sleeping, even during the sunup hours. Slumber became more a thing of inconvenience, a waste of time that could be spent hungering and burning inside. His eyes were scabbed fruit pressed into the sockets of a skull. It was like looking through scales. If he blinked, they would crack, inviting clear fluid that would dribble down his gaunt cheeks. He licked them free with his long, thin tongue. Tears were another precious liquid, just as delicious. The stink in the trailer was so potent, you could almost see it, a reeking haze that hung in the stale air. He stood in the corner of the disused bedroom. The standing wardrobe had been angled to create a corner devoid of almost any light at all. He stood, pressed into that corner like a statue. In the darkness, his stomach growled, and it sounded like a dog ready to attack.

The Mouth tilted his long neck, and the bones beneath the pallid skin cracked and popped like wood in a fire. His belly snarled again, and he dragged shaking, long fingers down his shirtless torso. He let the points of his fingernails dance over the ridged edge of the swollen sore that was making itself at home there. The welt began at his sternum and ran down to where a navel should have been. The puffy skin was hot and soft, it gave like risen dough under his touch. He pushed until he felt wet on his fingers. The Mouth winced and smiled. This was pleasing.

He was becoming.

More accurately, a home-becoming. Were there not so many thin teeth in the way, he would have laughed or even smiled at his silly pun. Along his spine, nerves whistled and laughed. In his fevered brain, one small voice had taken the lead. It was becoming clearer in its requests, its demands. For a miniscule second, he recalled life before he was The Mouth, but like a flea on summer skin, it was smacked away.

In the corner, in the thick shadows of late day, The Mouth put his large hands over his open eyes and let the dark corner swaddle him and kiss him all over as he rested.

26

"You're home fairly early,"
Elijah's mother was sitting at the small dinette table in the kitchen. The smoke from her Marlboro doodling swirls in the air over her head. Her other hand rested on the handle of her coffee cup.

"Tierny was busy, and Ken was having a bad day. Well, mostly a good day, but it went bad this afternoon."

"Honey, it's not going to get better. The bad days and moments will flip the board and you'll be saying things like Ken had a good day. That will become a rarity."

Elijah slid into the chair and sat across from his mother. She hadn't slept much or at all. He could tell. The bags under her eyes were storm cloud dark. She made an attempt to smile and he returned his own. Xerox of a Xerox of a Xerox quality.

"Honey. I know you have trouble getting on with kids your age. Hell, I know there are only a few kids your age left in town. No one moves in but they sure find the way out. I know you say they all think you're weird for liking the stuff you do, but, I think you need to try and find some friends. Friends that aren't grown-ups."

Elijah opened his mouth to protest, but his mother held up her hand with the cigarette, her index finger pointing to the ceiling and stopping him mid outburst.

"I'm not saying you can't be friends with Tierny and Ken. Tierny is family; his sister married your Uncle Benny. And Ken, he's a sweet old man with no family or anyone to care about him, and I consider you a blessing to him. I'd never make you quit that. I'd never even ask that, but honey, there's a lot of pain headed your way. I think...I think you'd be better equipped to handle it when it happens, if you had some shoulders closer to your age and height to cry on."

The cigarette met her lips and the end winced red as she drew a breath through it. He heard the crinkly sound of the tobacco burning inside. He held his tongue and knew everything she said had been true. He watched her, tendrils of smoke floated from her small nostrils. For some reason, it made him think of the old Bible story where the hand writes on the wall.

"Thanks, Ma. I get it," was what he settled on.

She smiled. It was lopsided and did not meet her weary eyes. She stubbed out her smoke in the ashtray he had made her in art class in third grade, and stood up, stretching, causing her spine to pop. Elijah watched a thin pencil line of smoke rising from the butt in the ashtray.

"I'm going to try and lay down again. I work the bar tonight at six, until closing at two. I'll never make it if I don't sleep a little. Those jerks see that I'm beat, and they'll eat me alive with their bullshit."

Elijah paused and then went to her. He was as tall as she was now. He smiled and wrapped his arms around her and held her tight. She squeezed back hard enough to crack his back.

"I love you," he said in her ear, and he felt her chest hitch. He heard her sniffle and felt tears on his neck.

"I love you too, my sweet smart boy."

Across the street a dog barked. A truck drove by in need of exhaust work. Someone in the yard next door shouted at the barking dog. Through the cacophony, they did not break their embrace. It was a few minutes before his mother pulled away and wiped her wet eyes with a thumb, smearing the eyeliner like rained-on love letters.

"Thanks, I needed that," she said, then laughed and went into the living room. He heard the creak of the fourth step as she went upstairs.

He stood in the kitchen and replayed what had just happened in his mind. He would rewind and remember that moment for the rest of his life, with smiles that he would later trade for tears.

27

"Paula is never late." Holly was in a snit. She held her car keys in hands tipped with bright blue nails. She leaned on the counter and stared at Tierny who was sitting at the desk looking at the dozen sticky notes that were plastered all over the printer, phone, and pen holder. Why the girl couldn't just write up a normal note was one of life's great mysteries. She never thought in a linear fashion. Bursts and stammers were the language of her brain. Tierny refocused on her nonstop bitching and held up a hand to silence her.

"Holly, just go. I'm sure she'll pull in as you're pulling out. No need to get your knickers in a twist. I can handle this desk for a while. I've done it before. It isn't difficult."

Holly smiled and made for the door.

"Thanks, Tier," she offered over a shoulder before stopping at the door and boomeranging back to the desk. "I'm not mad, I'm worried. She's never this late, you know. I'm gonna swing by her place and make sure she's okay. Might've just overslept."

"Go ahead and do that. I'm sure that's the case. Tell her not to kill herself rushing. I've got this."

Holly stormed out into the morning light, immediately cutting its brightness with a hand above her eyes. Tierny smirked, as she disappeared from his line of sight. He plucked sticky notes from where they hung and went about logging them all on a piece of paper.

A coherent list, imagine that.

It was almost a half hour later and he had managed to get the fourteenth note transcribed by the time the phone rang. He looked at the number on the display and recognized it as he cleared his throat and put his voice into its deepest setting.

"Howdy. This is Bad Brad Tierny, thanks for calling the International House of Wrinkles."

"Oh my God! Tier? Tier! Paula's dead. She's..."

He could barely make out anything she said after that. Her voice was keening and shrill. He could barely hear it. She must have had the landline phone stretched as far as the cord would reach. There was static mixing with her sobs. But Tierny wasn't listening anymore. He sat there at the desk as icy numbness filled his guts. He held the receiver in his hand, and after Holly hung up, the line eventually went to a droning ringtone.

He sat like that, his fingers threatening to cramp in their tight grip of the receiver, until he heard the sirens moving through town and knew that it was real.

28

There was a sign on the door that was neat but hastily written that said *No Visitors Today*, in sloping black marker. Not the most professional, but what does grief know about decorum?

Elijah had watched the fill-in nurse, a short rotund lady from the medical center, on the other side of the mountain, tape it up earlier.

Now, he sat on a folding chair on his porch and stared at the facility. Thought of the old people sleeping in its belly, unaware that one that had taken care of them was gone. Just waiting for this day to roll into the next, and the one after that, and the next. Time was elastic, stretchy but taut, until you became elderly. Then, when you are at your least steady, it was a tightrope, a razor blade's edge.

Elijah found his gaze wandering to the parking lot. He specifically eyed the last spot before the hedge, where Paula had always parked her blue Dodge Shadow, with the faded bumper sticker about the Air Force holding a bake sale to buy a bomber. The stupid pink fuzzy dice hanging from the rearview mirror. He smiled as he recalled the times she gave him a ride to the store on a day when it was raining. She made him buckle his seatbelt before she would even turn the key, even though she did not wear hers. There was junk all over the back seat. Jackets, sweatshirts, papers, and candy wrappers. Her car smelled like bubblegum and hairspray. They had listened to the radio, and she sang along to whatever came on. She had waited while he bought the stuff on his mom's list and drove him back, even though he told her he could leg it. She was nice. To him. To the patients. To everyone.

He turned and went back into the house to wait for his mother to come down. The clock on the microwave had it at quarter of twelve, the service would be starting in forty-five minutes. He breathed in and sighed as he fondled the bottom edge of his suit coat, worrying the small thread that barely peeked from the lining. His mother had said he could just wear a button-down shirt and nice jeans, but he wanted to be a grown up today. He wanted to walk among men and women as though he were one of them. Full of anger, aching, and insecurity, but hiding it all behind a fake smile and under a spiffy suit, just like a grown up.

29

"The shit about the veins and arteries and all that being gone as well as the blood, that was bull-shit. Significant blood loss, yes. Throats torn open, yes, but the means of travel for the red stuff was intact. There was almost no blood left in the bodies. That is also a fact."

Tierny sat at the table hunched forward, facing Elijah. They spoke in hushed voices. The boy had the notebook open, and his pen was moving swiftly. After a few minutes it stopped, and Elijah looked up from his transcription.

"How did you find that out?"

Tierny made a face somewhere between a grimace and a smirk before he answered.

"I went to school with the coroner's assistant over in Steelwater. We've gone out two or three times, so I called and asked him to meet me for a beer last night and I got it out of him."

"Why would Marty tell Mr. Scott if it wasn't true."

"It's just a thing people do. Adults, but everyone, really. They hear something and want to further the chain of gossip, but they also want to give it more importance, more oomph so it's theirs now to hold until they pass it on, so they dress it in frills and fallacy and then lob it into the hands of the next person, who does the same damn thing. Hell, I've done it myself."

"Adults are fucking weird." Elijah remarked softly as he added another sentence to his notes.

"Language." Tierny said and shook a finger at the boy, like an old school marm. Elijah stuck out his tongue and the moment of levity evaporated. The two sat in the recreation room, where they whispered and wrote things down while the television showed *Mama's Family* with the volume off.

"So, this brings the total to five."

Tierny nodded, but then he stole a glance at the doorway to secure their privacy. He pulled out a piece of lined paper. The writing on it was very neat, not Tierny's for sure.

"Kyle also gave me this. These ones highlighted in yellow, are three other murders, well, suspicious deaths, in neighboring counties. These, the ones in pink, that's another four from further out, across the state line. And so on...there's a string of these killings that go out to the edge of Ohio. The gaps in time and distance between locations kept them from being pegged as connected. They go back for a couple of years. There are lulls. Kyle was intrigued by our sleuthing... or well, whatever we're doing."

"Why the breaks?"

"I'm thinking our man needs to rest. I'm thinking what he's doing takes a considerable toll on him and rest is important."

"As far as whatever we're doing, all we've done is logged all the facts about the murders,

like, just copied from the stupid papers and Ken's weird

rambling. We need to find a suspect and watch them or look for clues. Something like that. This is not going to win us any press awards." Elijah seemed proud of his snark, but Tierny ignored it, and now it was the boy's turn to know the heartbreak of missed humor.

"I have an idea. Meet me here tonight around seven. Your mom works tonight, yeah?"

Elijah nodded. "She's at the bar until like one or two."

"Okay, meet me here, bring a flashlight and some gloves." Tierny paused. "I mean like dishwashing gloves or rubber ones, not your Freezy Freakies."

Elijah just nodded; another Tierny joke felled by youth. The bearded man sighed and stood up from the table.

"I gotta dispense pills and cheer. See you later."

"Think I could visit Ken a little?"

"Afraid not, little buddy, he's having a bad day. He's just sleeping, and he was agitated and somewhat combative this morning. Let him have the day to rest."

The boy nodded. He slid the pen and tablet into his bag and followed Tierny to the door. They high fived and parted company.

Down at the end of the hall, Ken slept in his room. His hands gripped the edge of the blanket, knuckles white. His lips moved, and low, soft mutterings scurried from them. He mumbled about his mother and his wives. About children long deceased, about balloons and brothers and angry, hungry mouths.

30

The Mouth was nearly complete. He stood in the corner behind the wardrobe. The room was dim and buzzed with flies. His white skin was slicked with heavy sweat and blood that was his own. He had pulled the full-length mirror from the back of the bathroom door and had it leaning against the wall before him.

He smiled with all his being. The wound that had formed down the length of his torso was open. The edges were swollen and raw, they wept a thick ichor. He allowed his fingers to dance along the raised edge. He slipped them inside the opening and the wound closed softly over them. His fingertips felt sharp triangles, felt smooth wet tissue. The teeth inside pricked his fingers, and he felt the skin break. There were pulsating contractions of muscle as his body mouth suckled his wounded digits. He filled with raw electricity as he cannibalized–*no*, recycled— himself to build his true being. He gazed down at the rolling movement of his body mouth and allowed his free hand to feel lower than that, to find the hardest part of him and grasp it with a slick, wet hand and yank it awake.

His breathing did not change, nor did his physical demeanor, as he pulled himself along with quick, rough movements. Breathing in hot bursts from his nose, feeling small licks of sour breath on the back of his hand from his body mouth. He kept at it and did so to completion, spilling curdled, red-tinged seed up into the waiting mouth of his stomach. He swallowed eagerly, and when he felt the rough tongue snake out and swab the area where he had spurted, he felt a surge in the roiling power within him. He heard cracking sounds as his ribs shifted to make room for the gullet that would be needed, one that would reach through his body into dark corners of being that went beyond flesh and physiology. Beyond even time and rationality. The cavernous realm where the things that made the voices resided. Where the shadow child stood behind the myriad of dark ones and waited patiently.

The Mouth fed from himself; in the dark womb he had created. He fed and changed and waited, ready to be reborn.

31

"Good morning, Ken. Look who popped by to see you." Tierny was loud but not shouting. The old man opened his eyes, but the weak light in the room was still enough to reduce them to nearly closed slits. Ken looked towards the dark rectangle that was the doorway and saw Elijah standing there, his satchel slung over a shoulder.

"Who are you?" Ken asked, and the absence of recognition in his eyes and voice hurt the boy like a brick to the knee.

"It's me, Elijah." He also raised his voice. The conversation stalled there for a few minutes. Ken roused and pulled himself up into more of a sitting position. He picked up the pair of glasses on his side table and slid them onto his thin face.

"Oh, Elijah, my boy. How are you?" He was smiling now, the curtain of his malady pulled aside that quickly.

"I'm ok. I missed you the last few days. Tier said I needed to let you rest."

"Since when do we listen to the bearded one? My boy,

how you've grown. I'd say at least an inch since last I saw you."

The old man winked behind his specs and Elijah felt the sting from earlier fade. He knew it was short lived. That there would come a day when the forgetting would be permanent. He would just be a page in a cumbersome book in the old man's lap that he had forgotten how to read. He took the slender, wrinkled hand of his friend and squeezed it. He nodded and smiled. Today is often the best gift we have, and he was going to do his best to remember that. He looked over and nodded at Tierny who returned it and gave the man in the bed a small salute and left, the door closing behind him.

"So boy, tell me what is new in your world."

"You heard about Paula, right?"

The look that washed over Ken's face was a cloud in a clear sky. His thin lips went away, and his eyes grew damp. The old man sniffed and nodded.

"Yes. Dear, poor girl. He got to her. Senseless. I just don't see what he's getting at with this nonsense."

Elijah frowned at the old man talking like the killer was a petulant child in his care. He stayed quiet and allowed the man to continue.

"You give of yourself and build an existence for some-one, and they take that and they

bend it and they drag it to dark corners and drape it over shoulders hunched by anger and resentment and so much anguish, and then they get in with the wrong crowd and hoo boy..."

He became aware of the boy's stare and stopped speak-ing. A rasp of a chuckle escaped his wrinkled throat, and he waved his hand at the glass on the table. Elijah filled it from the pitcher and handed it to his friend. Ken sipped and put it down, smacking his lips.

"Forgive me boy, I was just...writing. I was writing in my head and forgot myself and spoke it aloud."

Ken slid back down into his bed and pulled the blanket up to his neck.

"I'm afraid I'm still a bit worn out. I'd like a small cat nap. Go prattle with Tierny and let me sleep a little longer. Let us meet this afternoon in the big room."

Elijah nodded and left the room without saying good-bye. Too busy trying to figure out what the hell had just happened. Once the door was closed, Ken pulled the blanket over his head and started to mumble to himself. If there had been anyone there to hear, it would have sounded like bickering.

32

"It was weird, man. Like he was just normal for a minute then he got all bizarre and started talking this shit about creating someone and them being mad and bitter...it was just crazy weirdo shit."

"Dude, I told you. Dementia has its hooks in him and things like this are normal. Normal in that nothing will be normal again. He'll slip from time in mid conversation. Start chatting with us now and the next time he talks it's thirty years ago and he has no inkling who we are. That's what it does. Dementia is like a giant mouth that just eats and eats until there's nothing left."

There was a lull after that and they both felt it, a sense of unease at the accuracy of that analogy.

"Ken wants to meet in the big room this afternoon. It's almost one now. Why don't you go home and eat lunch or go hang out with some kids your own age or watch one of your titty and blood movies and meet me back here at the desk at like three. I'll get Ken up and in the rec room. Hopefully, he stays sharp enough for us to ask some questions. I've got a suspicion we need to."

"What makes you say that?"

"I'll tell you then. Get out." Tierny pointed at the door and made an exaggerated angry face. Elijah shook his head and exited. He watched the kid cross the yard and climb the small hill to the road's edge, and then cross and walk to his front porch. Tierny smiled and turned back to the desk and found some work to do.

33

"Tierny's taking me to see that new *Cretin* movie. It's the fourth one and supposed to be the bloodiest."

"*Cretin*? That's a terrible name for a franchise." Elijah's mother had her back to him, dishes clinked in the sink as she rinsed them.

"The killer is like an inbred monster. He's not real sharp but he is mean. He usually kills people with a shovel or an ax. He's big and ugly."

His mother sighed and he knew even without seeing her face, she had rolled her eyes.

"I guess. But I swear, Tierny is just a thirteen-year-old trapped in a man's body. Have fun and call me at the bar when you get home so I don't worry. Regular rules apply. Nobody is in the house while I'm at work. Doors are all locked as soon as you get in. And in light of the ridiculous electric bill, I got in the mail yesterday, only lights in the room you're occupying, please."

"Okay." Elijah watched her pull off the dishwashing

gloves and drape them over the faucet before she walked over to the end of the table where her coffee cup waited.

"I gotta go get a power nap. It's about three. There's left-over lasagna in the fridge if your uncle-in-law doesn't spoil you with greasy burgers and fries."

She turned to give him a hug and tell him goodnight, and never noticed the gloves were no longer where she'd left them. As she stomped her way up the stairs, Elijah rifled through the junk drawer until he found one of the flash-lights. He checked it and upon finding it in working order, dropped it in his bag with the gloves. His stomach fluttered. He felt anxious and afraid and giddy at the same time, and he didn't even know what kind of plan Tierny was concoct-ing. He looked at the clock and hurried out the door.

34

"The new *Cretin* movie? Christ, boy. I've got better taste than that."

Tierny's face was red from laughing. He wiped his eyes and clamped a hand on the boy's shoulder.

"Honorable alibi though. A movie so dumb we can flat out freebase the plot and nobody would call it."

"I wanted something that would keep me off her radar for the night and not have her worrying."

"I hear you. Let's get to the rec room. I got Ken up and moving. He seemed pretty perky after Holly gave him his sponge bath, but who wouldn't be?" Tierny raised his eyebrows up and down.

"Please, Tier, I'm not an idiot. That idea does nothing for you."

There could have been a moment. There could have been serious discussion about lifestyles, preferences or proclivities and the way some folks are cut differently than others. But the simple beauty of the moment, the honest lack of care about distinctions and differences the boy showed felt like enough. Just the fact that they were friends and the bond was shared, loving and true, was as well. Tierny's chest grew warm as he let it pass.

Tierny cleared his throat, and they walked down the hall to the large room. Ken was sitting in the puffy recliner watching the television. The sound was off, but Lucy was shoving candy from a conveyor belt into her mouth, faster and faster she shoved, as the belt also sped up. There was probably a laugh track, but no humor reflected in the old man's features. He could have been carved from stone.

"Hiya Ken." Elijah piped up and the sound of his chipper voice cracked the ice encasing his elderly friend.

"My dear boy. How are you?" Ken was smiling and it seemed warm and real. But no less bothersome was the way he made it feel as though he had not seen Elijah in a very long time when it had in fact only been a couple of hours.

One day, it will be like he had never seen you at all, ever.

"I'm good, thanks for asking." Elijah pulled out one of the empty chairs and sat down. He hoisted his bag onto the table and removed its contents with a subdued flourish, a novice magician who wanted you to see what he was doing while trying his best to make like he was doing nothing at all. The notebook and pen. The newspapers. The flashlight and lemon colored rubber gloves. The old man's eyebrow arched, and he looked to Tierny who began to giggle.

"Oh man, I was kidding about the gloves, 'Li. I meant it about the flashlight, but the gloves were a joke."

"Why'd you want the flashlight then?"

"I thought we might go snooping around at some point."

You're a dick, Elijah mouthed across the table. Tierny wound down his laughter and looked at Ken.

"I have a friend who works with the coroner's office. He gave us some information. It's in the notebook with ours. He found other murders, same in style, they trace out all the way to the far border of Ohio. The first being unique in that it is reported and followed only as a missing person. Some fella named Randy, I think. He was some kind of loner who wanted as little to do with society as possible. Built and lived in a little shack. Scavenged for stuff he sold to buy things he couldn't manage for himself. He was a real Grizzly Adams kinda fella...without the bear."

Ken nodded. His eyes were narrow, focused. He was still along for the ride, so Tierny continued.

"There are several more, spanning a few years, dotting the counties from there to, well, right here. Now. It's a definite path on the map, not exactly from point A to point B, but it's a line nonetheless. It's no straight shot but more ragged like..."

"A wound." Ken's voice was as sure as it had sounded in weeks.

Ken's eyes had widened, a little, the tip of his tongue wetting dry lips as he prepared to speak. Elijah grabbed the pen and opened the notebook to the first blank page.

35

The Mouth dropped his hands away from eyes that were clotted with brittle golden crust. It yawned—wide—and from the cavern of its throat, faces leered and screamed. Its needle teeth pricked dry lips. In its chest, furred things rolled and gnashed their teeth. The chasm of its stomach yearned with a hunger as deep as biblical promise. The creature stretched and new bones bent and crackled like burning kindling. Old flesh split and wept. Skin parted like lips to whisper. To sing. To proclaim.

It breathed deeply and something that might have been a smile grew. A wicked upward slash, erupting with bright new teeth. Sharp and eager. The Mouth listened as the chorus of voices in its head rallied and hooted in raucous celebration. It was time. He—they— were home. In the shadows of its heart, Vestus held the hands of the larger darker ones, the ones who had been there and nurtured him, had carried him on crooked shoulders. The one that wore Grandmother's face feigned niceties better than the rest. Their hands of tar and obsidian had held and caressed him these endless years. The Mouth smiled when they congratulated him on his homecoming. When they serenaded him with an agonized chorus, the smile grew until the wet mouth touched the corners of large, eggy eyes.

Every child seeks accolades.

36

"I was born in Ohio. It was the same day as independence..." His voice was old paper that threatened to crumble if held.

Tierny forgot all about the humor of moments ago. He felt a sadness build as he realized what the old man was saying. He looked to the boy who was writing it down anyway, but the look on his young face showed that it had not been lost on him, either. He was doing his book thing. Elijah sighed and the pen in his hand stilled. *Oh no*, he thought.

"My brother was unborn that very day. He slid through behind me but whereas I sucked precious breath and then nipple, his wide lipless mouth sucked nil and the only bosom he would know was that of darkness and black flame. Can you imagine being born and erased at the same time? The one that carried you, that *made* you, being horrified by you? That betrayal must transcend, I'd fathom. I believe that ripple to be a wave felt through planes of being. He must've been so alone in his darkness. So very lonely and afraid, until anger came to call. No stronger and more dangerous trinity has there been, eh?"

Elijah stopped writing again and looked at Tierny whose mouth had dropped open, slightly,

"Ken. What are you thinking?" Elijah spoke slowly and kept his anxious voice even.

"I think my brother has found a way. I believe that he has shucked the dark cowl that has shrouded his unbeing. He waited in blackness with all that anger and all that bitterness and then, he found friends. Found the darkest kind of family and they helped him grow until he found a way out. *Through.* A door as small as a bottleneck. Resurrection is as simple as walking a camel through the needle's eye, they say."

His chuckle was loose and sharp at the edges. His eyes watered and his hands were trembling.

Elijah realized that Ken wasn't thinking this, not just now, maybe never. He knew it to be the truth. He looked at Tierny and tilted his head. Tierny stood and walked to where the boy was sitting. Ken paid them no mind, just stared at the tabletop like it were a Seer's stone.

"I think he knows that's what's going on. I know it sounds bonkers, but he feels it to be true. He means what he's saying...thinking. I think he's been *feeling* it." Elijah whispered it all in a rush.

"It really isn't that far off from the shit in that book I was reading. What if, his brother's spirit, ghost, whatever, gets lost in..." Tierny paused and looked at Ken.

"Ken? How did Vestus get to the dark place? You said the doctor had burned him."

Ken smiled a half smile. "Heh. Just his little body, son, just the meat and bones. Just the cage." He swallowed hard before he continued.

"Grandmother had freed him well before that, my friend. She gave him the bottle and the gift of flight. She was sending him to the heavens but..."

His eyes teared again and his voice cracked.

"An impatient boy. A fidgety whelp. I was supposed to wait for a precise time, but I let go of the balloon. Too soon. I let my brother run away. The baited line pulled through the ripples of night..."

Tierny left the old man rambling while he leaned closer to the boy, they were conspirators to anyone looking.

"So... his dead brother's spirit, soul, something, is put in a bottle, tied to a balloon, and was meant to be released at a given time. Probably some sort of ritual thing his grandma was doing. He lets it go too early, so instead of making it to where it was meant to go, he is in another place, but still part of this one. The bottle--it's corporeal so it stays in our world--gets lost somewhere when the balloon pops or deflates." He stopped speaking and just stared and nodded as he stitched together the rest of the crackpot scenario. Tierny started again.

"The dead brother's soul is trapped in the bottle here until someone finds it. Our Randy hobo fella. He finds a cool old bottle and takes it home and opens it..."

"The recluse, dude. It's opening a bottle and his ghost or whatever comes out, but, I think, that bottle is just a doorway for him. Them...it. When Vestus was in it, he was in some darker place. The void. I don't quite know. But just to *him*. The spirit thing. He's just been in limbo or something, he's been in the waiting room world." Elijah grabs a thread and pulls himself into the idea they are concocting.

"Of Hell or whatever afterlife there is? I don't know." Tierny said it, and it sounded melodramatic but right.

"This is some wild and crazy shit, Tier. We're living the

worst exposition scene ever. Maybe my mom was right, and we do watch too many horror movies." Elijah paused and looked at Ken who was nodding and whispering what seemed to be gibberish.

"Ken, why is he looking for you, do you think?" Elijah asked. The old man seemed to respond better to him.

"I was never easy to find. I've moved and hid my whole life. Behind wives and names. In cities and towns. But I'm slow now. The horse is lame, and he knows it. Because I got what he did not. I got his life, too. I've lived two very long lifetimes and they're coming to an end. He wants to make me pay for that...like a coin. Two sides we were...are. The shadow I cast has always been his."

The old man laughed like the bark of a mad dog.

37

"Ken is in bed. He was all worked up, shaking and muttering, and he didn't seem to know me. I gave him some sedation and got him laid down. He went out almost as soon as his head hit the pillow. I got Holly to have the night nurse keep an eye on him until we get back." Tierny swung the key ring around on his finger while he and Elijah walked across the grass to the lot. The sun was nearly absent, and the moon paced the side of the stage.

"It's disturbing how that happens with him. He was so talkative and animated, and then it's like, the strings were snipped and he's barely with it." Elijah sat in the passenger seat as Tierny pulled open the driver's side door.

"I told you, that's how it is with his condition. But I think this is more an exhaustion catching up to him. Like a soul deep fatigue. I'm not at all sure what the fuck I'm thinking at the moment."

"Language." The boy admonished.

"Pfft. I think the whole idea we just cobbled together is some grade A, B-movie, nonsense. I think we're nuts to even entertain it. But my gut says it's also the truth or really fucking close to it. This whole thing has just had a certain feel to it from the get-go. I can't really speak to it properly, but I'm thinking it might be a two-fold dilemma. I'm thinking that all the shit about the witchy grandma and the deformed brother and the bungled ritual and all that might be true. But I'm wondering if maybe it isn't also something like an old story I read. I think it was called *Mannikins of Horror*. Robert Bloch wrote it, and it was an episode on one of them old thriller shows. It was about a doctor who lost his mind a bit, started making these little clay figures and he sort of willed them to life and they did his bidding. I don't think he was initially aware he was doing it. I was little and not supposed to be up that late watching shit like that. So, I'm sure I missed bits trying to keep hidden behind the end of the couch at the end of the living room."

"So maybe Ken *called* him to him. Not on purpose. Maybe not even aware in any way. Maybe his dementia kinda stopped cloaking some kind of link they shared being twins."

"Yeah. I've read lots of stuff about psychic links with twins. Not at all sure why they'd need to be alive. Kind of a reverse Cheng and Eng situation, ya know, except for the being conjoined part."

Elijah nodded even though he had no clue who those names belonged to or why Tierny had mentioned them. He was about to respond with something stupid when the shadow pulled itself from the growing dark nesting at the corner where the lot merged with the woods. It fell over the windshield, and he heard the sound of Tierny's keys hitting the macadam.

38

The thing that stood before the car might have been a man at one time. It looked more like an effigy whittled from a madman's memory. Wrong proportions, drenched in nightmare. The creature was tall, but not naturally so. Its legs were more than half its height and they were not straight. They bent oddly at too many joints, like warped stilts made by an amateur. The tattered cuffs of filthy jeans hung about where a knee should have been. Shoeless feet were tipped in nails that curled like talons, thick and yellowed.

Elijah remained frozen in the passenger seat, straining to take in the full monstrosity before them. Tierny stood still with his hand on the door handle. Keys at his feet, forgotten already.

The man-thing placed its long hands on the hood of the car, arms so long as to allow it to remain fully upright while doing so.

"My God." Tierny muttered when he saw the cleft that ran the length of the thing's torso. A vaginal-looking orifice that drooled thick clear liquid and was rimmed with sharp points the size of thumbs. Blazing white against the bruise-colored flesh beneath and around. It dropped its head down lower than its chest, on a neck that seemed too long to be able to bear the weight of such a head. Enormous eyes glowed the sunny yellow of egg yolks on a breakfast plate. They were off center and took up space normally assigned to cheekbones. They oozed thick white goo from the corners, that marred the remaining flesh of its cheeks like melted candle wax. The nose was nearly absent, filling in were two bubbling holes beneath the eyes. Even the horror of all that paled in comparison to the mouth that occupied the bottom of the face. It was a ragged chasm rent with a dull, broken blade. A jack-o-lantern carved by a spastic. It spread from ear to ear and practically hinged its head. It opened wide enough to show off the teeth that cascaded over shredded lips in a waterfall that promised only pain and agony.

It stood and stared at the two. A strange sound came from its mouth, almost like a tea kettle before it was fully ready to whistle. It sounded like a chorus of whispers. Tierny glanced down and noted his keys were right by his foot. He hissed low through his teeth and Elijah looked at him. The kid was rightfully terrified. Tierny gave a quick nod and darted his eyes downward to show the boy the spot where the keys had landed. Tierny licked his lips.

"One." He said and disguised it as a heavy breath he had exhaled. The beast did not move. Just stared at them with those large eyes.

"Two."

Elijah slowly slid across the seat, his arm stretching out and downward until his fingers felt the cool metal of the ring of keys. He looked up into Tierny's sweaty face and pulled his hand back with the keys, slow and quiet. Tierny subtly half crouched and moved a little closer to the open driver's seat. He held out a hand for the boy to give over the keys. The jingle when they hit his palm snapped the creature from its daze. It cocked its head as it stood up to full height, blocking the newly risen moon from view. Both Tierny and Elijah screamed as the key turned and the engine came to life.

In the bright light of the headlights, the side door of the building opened with its squeaking and the monster swiveled quickly to see who had interrupted the bizarre standoff.

"Oh shit."

The words fell out of Tierny's mouth with barely any inflection at all. He and Elijah watched as Holly danced her way out into the parking lot. Headphones over her ears and her eyes on the ground. The monster started off in her direction.

39

Tierny stomped his foot down as hard as he could, and the truck roared forward and the thing was just steps ahead when the pick-up stopped. The engine still grumbled but the vehicle just sat there. Tierny pushed the gas pedal and the engine growled louder but the truck seemed to want to move but did not.

Tierny shook his head and opened the door, jumped out and paused to confirm his worst suspicion. He didn't have time to sigh or be embarrassed. He had driven over the concrete parking space bumper and his truck was low enough that it had effectively snagged the undercarriage of the vehicle. He saw the red puddle of transmission fluid beginning to pool near where he stood, like fresh blood. The truck was bleeding out.

"Move it, boy!" he hollered, and he reached behind the seat, grabbed something from the back seat.

Elijah cowered next to the facility van that occupied the neighboring spot when he saw Tierny approach the creature with his arms raised high overhead, and were the situation not so terrifying, the ridiculousness might have made him laugh.

Tierny swung a hockey stick down and around as hard as he could. A lifetime of ridicule and sadness and whatever else burned like jet fuel for his muscles. He screamed and the monster opened its enormous mouth and turned away from the still hapless Holly. The blade of the stick connected with the side of its lumpen head and obliterated one of its eyes. The membrane splitting to allow a geyser of fluid spurt in a way that made Elijah think of popping pimples.

The Vestus thing screeched and surged forward at Tierny, who was rearing back for another swing. Tierny bellowed once more and delivered a swing that stopped in one giant hand of the beast in front of him. The noise that came from that terrifying mouth was almost a chuckle. Layered by the many voices that harmonized to create it. The sound made Tierny piss his pants.

40

Her scream was power metal, high and piercing. It soared above them in the night. Holly had finally looked up from her dancing and saw the scene in the parking lot. She pulled the headphones from her ears and let them dangle like futuristic fashion jewelry. She did not move. She hardly breathed. A fist of terror squeezed her into a statue. A sickly almost quiet fell over the parking lot. Tierny's ragged breathing, Elijah's crying, and whatever that low growling noise from the creature, the only sounds. The thing held a hockey stick in its big hands and in one quick burst of motion, snapped it as though it were made of balsa wood. The straight end fell to the ground with a clatter as the beast turned the blade end around to point the splintered, spear-like end at Tierny.

Tierny looked to Elijah and yelled again. "Fucking move, Kid!"

Elijah heard and put on a burst of speed that got him as far as Holly, who threw her arms around him in mid-crouch and rapidly backwards walked them to the door she had come out of. Tierny blew a breath out and sucked in another deeper one. He gave the boy a quick nod and bolted. He blew past the monster and was just past the front of the van, five or six yards from Holly and Elijah in an instant. He pumped his out of shape legs and felt the muscles in them burning. Felt his lungs cursing him for feeding them smoke all these years. His eyes streamed tears and he ran as hard as he could. He got to the door and Holly flung it open and Elijah took his hand to pull him in to safety,

"I'm here. I'm here." Tierny gasped in heaving breaths as he stepped onto the cusp of the doorway. He grabbed the door's edge to slam it behind him as the end of the hockey stick erupted from his upper stomach. The splintered point pushed out shredded muscle and fat. spraying the faces of his screaming friends with warm blood. Tierny winced and turned using the remaining strength he had to force the door closed and get the deadbolt in place. He sank to his knees, slid backwards against the wall, a growing puddle of his own creation spreading around him, and closed his eyes for a second.

Elijah held his canvas bag against Tierny's wound. Pushed it in and down with all his strength and sobbed while Holly ran to the desk. She whimpered as she held the phone in her trembling hand and tried to configure the buttons with her other shaking hand. Tierny looked up into the kid's swollen eyes and managed a smile. He spoke as calmly as he could.

"Elijah."

He punctuated the word with a labored breath that smelled meaty. The boy saw that his friend's chin and beard were glazed with dark droplets. Tierny held a hand out to the boy, who took it with his own.

"This...not planned..." The man forced a chuckle that

sounded like grinding gears. Behind him, the door shook, but the lock held. The door quaked again.

"Tier. Stay still and quiet. Holly called the ambulance." Elijah spoke soft but firm, trying hard to sound adult. He smiled at his older friend and squeezed the man's hand. He looked at Holly and she wasn't talking; she was just holding the phone and crying. He watched her push a button and start punching others in rapid succession.

"Okay. This is the hokey part. Listen... You're a good...young man. Gonna be an

amazing ...man...so smart and the care you have for people. 'Li... do great things... Anything... Everything." His weak smile faltered and the blood that was trickling from the corners of his mouth grew thicker, darker. "Just allow yourself... to do them...'Li... Don't rot here. Promise...the...this world is for you. I'll be watching you, so don't screw up..." His eyelids drooped and Elijah saw that the whites were shot through with bright red. He squeezed his friend's hand and leaned into the bag harder, hoping to miraculously staunch the tide of life that was pouring from Tierny.

The man attempted to laugh as he coughed up thicker matter that covered his chin. He squeezed the boy's hand and nodded at him. Elijah leaned his head against the top of the man's, he tried to hold the bag against the wound and embrace his friend at the same time. He cried loudly and his dying friend managed to lay his own head against the top of the boy's arm. Then the breathing stopped. Tierny sat still against the stupid owl statue that was by the door. Elijah cried like he hadn't done in years. He turned to see Holly was crying herself. The phone on the floor. She saw the kid looking at her and shook her head slowly. He crawled over to her, and she held him in the dark.

41

It had been nearly fifteen minutes when Elijah realized the noises from outside had ceased. The door was still there and there were no roars or any other sounds disturbing the night. He reached for the phone where it lay by the desk chair, but Holly grabbed his hand.

"It won't go through. It lets you dial but it won't ring and then it just kicks you back to a dial tone." She looked over by the door where Tierny's body leaned, propped against the owl statue.

"I'm sorry." She broke down into tears again.

Elijah grabbed her arm and pulled until she looked at him.

"That thing is here for Ken. I'm not sure what it wants but it's been looking for him for a long time and it's not happy. We gotta get him outta here."

Holly nodded and they stood up. They looked back in the direction of the door before slinking down the hall to Ken's room. The door was slightly ajar, inside nothing seemed to move and all was quiet save for the rapid snores of the old man. Elijah pushed the door all the way open and slid his hand down the wall until it hit the switch and there was a burst of light. The old man stayed asleep. His mouth moved nonstop like he was delivering a litany.

The boy crept to his bedside and laid a hand on the old man's shoulder, giving it a light squeeze. Ken's eyes popped open like some mechanical action. His mouth stopped mid-whisper and he looked around the room, taking in his surroundings and the people with him. He looked at Holly who offered a feeble wave. Her make-up was a mess, she looked like a panda bear painted by a drunkard. Ken moved his gaze to the boy right beside him. He stared for an endless minute; his brows sloped in consternation.

"Who are you?" His voice was frail. It seemed to belong to someone else, like hearing the sea in a shell. Illusory.

Elijah's heart sank. After everything else, he didn't need this as well. He had lost one of his best friends, he didn't want to lose another right now.

"It's me, Ken. Elijah."

Ken stared at him, and his teeth clenched as he seemed to wrestle with something internally. His hands were clasped together as in prayer but the force they were sparring each other with caused veins to stand out in liver-spotted relief. Old nostrils flared and

Ken muttered a succession of the word *No*.

The boy looked to Holly, who hung her head and looked at the tile squares on the floor.

"Ken. C'mon. We need you here now. Please..." The kid's voice pleaded and betrayed him by cracking repeatedly during the short sentence. Hormones gave no fucks about seriousness of moment. The old man looked at him and his eyes softened, slowly. His lips stretched upwards into a smile. He reached out his hand and placed it on the boy's arm.

"Elijah. My boy. A little late for a visit, no?"

The boy began to feel a warmth spreading through him. The fact he was recognized was a good thing, but it seemed to be an innocent recognition. There was no gauge at all for taking in circumstances or surroundings. No notice for the fact he and Holly were obviously disheveled and had been crying, bloodstained and shaken. Ken patted the boy's arm affectionately.

"What's going on with you today, young man?" He smiled; his teeth seemed smaller in his pale gums. Elijah exhaled through his nose and wiped his free arm across his eyes. A red dirty smear ran down between his eyes like some kind of war paint.

"Ken. Listen carefully. It's Vestus. You know who that is?"

"Vestus? Vestus...oh, Vestus. My brother?" There was a look of alarm on his wrinkled face.

"Yeah, your brother. Do you remember Tierny and I talking with you about him earlier this afternoon? We were trying to figure out the murders."

At the mention of Tierny's name, a burning knot rose in the boy's throat. He felt more tears at the ready, but he swallowed them down. "C'mon Ken."

"I think I do. I told you of his birth and his death. And now he is born again. Not in the way of salvation, I fear. Never him." Ken made a ticking noise with his teeth and lips.

"He was lost. Awash in the darkness, and I provided a beacon, you see. I reached out to him. I extended the hand that held the branch that became a bridge. I was so...unwhole."

"What do you mean, Ken? Why did he kill those people if he was just trying to get to you?" Elijah felt inadequate asking the questions. He wished Tierny was there helping direct the interrogation.

"I let him go. The balloon. It was lost, his vessel, and he with it. But he was in the dark place. All alone. Until they came. Sniffed him out like hounds. They watched over him and taught him and kept him safe in their black cocoon. They tail him as shadow now. He is never alone."

The boy stole a look at Holly. She wore a look of total confusion mixed with the residual fear from earlier.

"His breadcrumb trail. That's all they were. He drank the blood because that's what I made him. He died before he ever lived, you see. He was a lot never thrown. I grew and gave him a body and a history and a story. I built him in my imagination, in fiction, but to him it was just a skin in a sense." Ken chuckled and it rasped like sandpaper.

"On purpose? You knew this would happen one day?"

"Oh no. I just wrote a book about a brother I never knew. All myths are seeds, boy. Every story, every parable is a stone in the foundation of being. A muscle in the shoulders of Atlas."

Ken was speaking with an assurance that Elijah had not seen in weeks.

Elijah grew impatient. He heard noises outside in the hall. He thought he heard the heavy thud of a door being knocked down. Holly moved over closer to the window.

"Ken. How do we stop him? He's a monster. He killed Tierny. He's going to kill us if we don't stop him." He looked behind him as the sound of splintering wood and breaking glass filled the hallway. "What do we do?" Elijah shook the old man, harder than he intended.

Ken's eyes dulled slightly. He looked to the doorway, where a large shadow was stretching along the wall. His eyes met the boy's.

"Oh, who are you? Where are we going?" He looked at Holly and smiled. "Pretty lady too."

Elijah felt something deflate inside of him. He turned and stuck his head out into the corridor where the Vestus-thing was still surveying the destruction of the nurse's center.

The other rooms were silent. Their occupants likely dozed with pharmaceutical assistance while the TVs stupe-fied them with reruns of Andy Griffith or Matlock. Elijah had an idea. He pulled out the drawer of Ken's dresser and began rummaging. Socks and pajamas fell to the floor as his nimble young fingers grasped and searched. He pulled out a worn book and a slender wooden box. The book was dogeared and the cover was barely hanging on, but that old pulpy cover was recognizable. A hint of teeth in the night sky. He flipped open the case and smiled at the contents: an old fountain pen, the sharp point of the nib catching light and throwing it across his wet eyes.

"What have you got there, boy?" Ken seemed simultane-ously curious and clueless. Elijah stepped toward the door and whispered to Holly.

"Stay with him. I think I have an idea, If I don't come back..." he shrugged and sidestepped into the hall.

"Elijah!" She called after.

42

The Vestus thing was standing less than five feet away when Elijah ran into the hall. He held the pen out in front of him like it was a switchblade. The creature stared at him with its remaining eye, the other still leaking strings of viscous fluid. The torso mouth gnashed its teeth and sent droplets of foamy drool all over the paneled walls. Elijah crouched lower and stayed alert. The monster took a step closer, and he saw that the teeth in its face-mouth were more like the quills of a porcupine just crammed in and on top of one another. The kid swallowed the slimy thing in his throat before he spoke.

"Vestus?"

"We are, I am, he is... here." The hideous head cocked to the side and the voice came from a mouth that never moved, like music from a tiny speaker.

"What are you here for? Your brother is not well."

"He is well enough for balance. He has lived and lived and lived while I have died and suckled rotten marrow and smoke for a long skinless time. It is my turn now. Ours. My brethren crave it too. They have carried and dragged me for so long. He knew this. He helped me. He made me from his own rib and his own breath. He created me with clay from his mind and breath from his heart. He wouldn't know how sour it would be in these lungs. How could he?"

That yellow eye blinked while the voice(s) fell from its mouth. Elijah tightened his grip on the pen and slowly stepped toward the nightmare.

"He can't know now. He is sick. He has a disease. It eats his memories and leaves him hollow. He wouldn't know you, not even if you weren't a monster." It took all his resolve to keep his voice steady, but Elijah managed it.

"He will know me. He knows me for I *am* he. He is the *you* in us, the we in me." It snaked out a thin worm of a tongue to swab cracked leaking lips.

"He will know me. He cannot deny." It stepped closer to the boy but kept its arms low at its sides. The belly mouth was still; mewling sounds dribbled from where the lips snagged on teeth.

"I can't let you see him. He's not well and he won't know you and it'll scare him to death."

"Exactly. It is my turn now. I... we have worked so hard to get here. To extinguish one flame and light a flame of my own. I will move into a new body. His. One I can care for and live in comfort for long years to come. I will travel and love and live. Really live. He has had enough time."

To Elijah's ears, he voice was still an unbalanced sync of voices but seemed to be slimming, becoming more singular and less of a chorus. The force that was Ken's brother was the one most in control, shedding the grip of the others that carried him upon pitch black shoulders. It placed a hand on the doorknob of Ken's door.

43

E lijah was terrified. His body was shaking so badly he could barely focus. Between the burning in his heart over the death of his friend and the fear that was close to smothering him, he fought to concentrate and try to defend his remaining friend. He drew in as deep a breath as he could and blew it out.

The kid launched himself at the beast. Hand out in front, swinging upward. The nib of the pen met the creature's remaining eye and punctured the membrane in a violent snag. The monster howled and brought the hand from the door up to cover the eye. Muffled by the door another scream mimicked that of the creature. Elijah pulled back and jabbed again. The point broke the thin skin of its shoulder. Rivulets of inky blood flowed down over its arm and torso. Elijah pulled back and stabbed repeatedly until the chest of the creature was punctured in at least a dozen places. It lost black blood and hissed angrily. Mirroring whimpers came from Ken's room. The blood rolled like mercury when it hit the floor. Like beetles beneath a garden stone, suddenly stunned by the sun's light. The Vestus thing swung out at the boy and the blow knocked Elijah to the floor.

Elijah landed on his butt and kicked out a leg to trip the blinded creature. Vestus tumbled against the door to Ken's room, feet slipping in the blood had not pilled and rolled away. It managed to turn the knob and the door opened slightly. Vestus turned and tried to walk but tripped again and landed against the door, pushing it wide enough to allow it to fall against the foot of the bed. It craned its long neck and tried to look for its brother with sightless eyes.

"Who are you?" Ken's voice was chipper. He could have been talking to anyone, certainly not a bleeding monster with a mouth down its torso. Not a creature born of loneliness, jealousy and grief of a thing it never had. Not his brother.

"Brother." The Vestus thing spoke, clear as water. There was almost a warmth in the voice. Beneath the word, whispers sighed and cheered. An audience unseen.

"Who is it? What are you doing in that?" Ken stretched forward, reaching for the arm of the creature across the foot of his bed. His trembling fingers met the mottled flesh of the monster's arm and gripped it, gently. The old man licked his lips and frowned. His eyes moistened as a look of sad concern settled upon his face.

"Are you hurt, sir? Shall I get some help?" Ken spoke in a reassuring manner, straining to lean forward. His hand gently patting the arm of the thing on his bed.

Elijah couldn't believe the scene. "Ken, it's the monster. The killer. It's..." The boy stepped forward and stretched his arm out to block the old man's reach.

The voice seemed to waft from the maw of the creature,

its mouth making no movements to allow for it. "I'm your brother. Vestus. I've come so far for you. So far and long."

Ken's face shifted. The sadness took root in his eyes, in the set of his mouth. He looked mournful. He squeezed the arm of the creature and nodded.

"I know. I know. I've waited. For so long."

"You owe me, brother. You have grieved and swam in guilt. You gave me *a* life...but you made me a monster." It squeezed Ken's shoulder hard enough that the claw-like nails broke the old man's thin skin. Red stains kissed through the fabric of his pajama shirt.

Ken let go of the arm and picked up the book that Elijah had laid on the edge of the bed. He opened it and tore the first page free from the binding.

"I can take it back. I can eat my words."

He crumpled it into his mouth and chewed slowly. Tears streamed down the old man's gaunt cheeks as his mouth worked.

"Ken? What the hell are you doing?" Elijah heard the volume of his voice and startled himself. He watched the creature lean forward, putting its weight on the arm on Ken's shoulder. It seemed to be weakening. The ruins of its eyes dripped down the angry flesh of its face.

The old man kept tore another page and pushed it into his mouth. The creature on the bed moaned. It was not an entirely mournful sound, but almost rapturous. The thing held its free hand over ruined eyes and remained still for the moment.

"A life flashing before my eyes, in reverse. Unliving, that which I never lived in the first place." Its bloody chest hitched, and it leaned forward, face inches from that of his brother. "It is the closest to life I have ever been," the words a shrinking whisper.

As he worked the tenth page into his mouth and chewed it, there was a sigh of almost relief from the facial mouth of the monster, as the one that split its chest howled. The myriad of yowls and voices shouting profane things and promises. One clearly called out treason. The monster winced and growled and crammed the arm that had been gripping Ken's shoulder into the protesting torso mouth. It began to chew, and the room filled with additional din, that of moist rending and crackling bone. Ken, cheeks wet with tears, choked down the book page he had been eating and fell back against the pillows, his distended stomach rose over to edge of the blanket.

The monster had eaten itself to the shoulder. The body mouth grinding mottled flesh with unholy teeth. It hunched forward and pushed itself deeper into the maw, "This is not at all as I had hoped. Expected." it barely breathed. It was fading. The skin faded to alabaster, a fungal pale complexion, rife with cracks like old china. Elijah stepped closer and drove the nib into the back of the creature's neck, the spot where the head joins. The skin gave and the implement slid in up to where the boy's fingers gripped it. Vestus groaned, tilting its face in the direction of the boy. "Your protection is noble. Your love for my brother. Any love for him. I expected little." A pause to allow a bloated bubble of inkish blood to flow from his mouth. "All these years. All the distance. All the rage. And... yet."

"Ken." Elijah's voice quivered. He wasn't sure what to say or do.

"Yes, Elijah. I'm...we're dying. He's dying...again."

"He thought he was going to get to be you."

The creature slumped forward, and the torso mouth growled at the interruption of the food supply. The shoulder stump sliding free and Vestus listing against the bedrail. "What I wanted." was the frail mumble that crawled from the creature's lips.

"The fool. He cannot be me when I was always him. Always." Ken said.

"You *ate* your book?"

"My words, boy, I ate my *words*. I brought him home. For the short time I have left, I shall be we. But I won't remember. He will be trapped in a room with blacked out windows. The life he fought so hard to take, flying away from carrion we, like a buzzard."

The old man smiled weakly and belched. Elijah looked down to where the monster was. Its ruined eyes dribbled thick liquid down gaunt cheeks. Its chest was weeping tarry blood from the dozens of holes Elijah had put there. The large mouth that ran down its chest was partly open and a yellow tongue hung from the bottom. The sinkhole stench of its breath buffeting his face like a septic breeze. It grew paler as Elijah watched. The whiteness gave way to near translucence until he saw nothing but suspicious stains on the comforter. He noticed Holly was gone and gave a frantic look around before she came back in from the hall.

"I was checking on the others. They're all sleeping in their rooms." She was twitchy and seemed unsure how to process all she had just seen. She started to cry again and tried to smile at the same time. "I'm going to go across the street to call someone. Cops. I'm not sure. What should I tell them?"

"Tell them whatever. It won't bring Tierny back. I'm going home. I want my mom." Elijah squeezed the old man's shoulder and leaned in for a hug. Ken squeezed back with no strength. Elijah left the room. Holly followed. Ken sat in the room, tears freely flowing and mumbled to himself. His thin fingers traced the sticky stains on his blanket.

"Who are you?" He said to no one. The door slowly moved and Ken peered into the shadows webbed behind it, before his wet eyes brightened.

"Oh, I've waited so long for you..."

E lijah stood alone at the mouth of the lane to the cemetery. He had his suit on, and the early autumn chill was kissing his cheeks and hands. He had told his mother he'd be right along. He needed a minute. He couldn't bring himself to go to the viewing and this was just as bad. All he could see was his friend's smiling eyes and that beard. He heard his laugh and smelled his cigarette breath. He sniffed back the tears that came.

He kicked at the stones on the ground when he heard the crunch of footsteps behind him.

"Elijah?" The voice was unfamiliar. Warm and sturdy.

He turned and saw the man walking toward him along the edge of the road, hands thrust deep in the pockets of his gray woolen coat.

"Yeah." He tried to sound mature and unintimidated, but recent events had worn him and he was fragile. He stepped toward the approaching fellow.

The man had reddish hair and a thin face. He had a beard that was flecked with gray and a sharp nose. He braced his hands on his knees and bent to look into Elijah's eyes.

"I'm Kyle. Brad...Tierny's spoken about you a lot." He held out a hand that was covered with freckles and Elijah took it and held it firm. He shook it twice but did not let it go.

"He told me about you. A little. Recently."

"Heh. Yeah. He was always...careful. Small towns, small minds and all." The man's smile was warm but frail. Elijah looked into his green eyes and smiled himself.

"He was the best, wasn't he?"

"Absolutely, he was." He licked his lips, and a small tear traced his cheek, taking a reddened path already marked. "He adored you; I just wanted you to know that."

"I know. I loved him."

"Me too. He was. an asshole sometimes...but he never lied. He didn't have a bad bone in his body."

"Nope. Never." I think I'm going to go in now." Elijah dropped the stick he'd been fiddling with and walked in the direction of the cemetery. Kyle followed.

"I hear you like horror movies. The dumb ones with red paint blood and boobs."

"Sure do. Do you?" Elijah found an edge of excitement creeping into his voice for the first time in several days.

"I... I never really watched them. I think I might try to learn to. Think you could help a geezer like me out?"

"I'm sure." They were about to the end of the graveyard. The cluster of folks gathered around the hole was several yards off. Elijah picked out his mother and gave her a small wave. She returned it discreetly. Elijah stopped and looked at his new friend.

"You go on, I'll be right there. I must do something first." The boy walked off down the row before him, until he came to the twisted trunk of an ancient willow tree. He looked down at the stone beneath its shade. At the freshly engraved words that lived there.

Kenneth Vestus Allenwood Born long ago.

Son, Brother, Husband, Friend

"Ken. I just wanted to say hello. They're burying Tierny today. After weeks of bullshit. I wanted to tell you I miss you. And I don't blame you. I don't think Tier does either. But I'm sure you've seen him, and you guys are causing some ruckus up there or wherever." He stood up and stuck his hand inside his suit pocket and it came out clutching the old fountain pen. The boy knelt on damp ground and placed it in the grass before the stone.

"I love you, Ken. Get to writing."

He rose and brushed off the knees of his suit pants and then took his place beside his mother. Kyle stood behind them. Elijah looked back over his shoulder and the man smiled at him. He saw Holly standing across from them, next to Mr. Scott and several other townspeople. He looked up at his mother and she dabbed at the corners of her eyes with her handkerchief. Elijah looked at the sun in the sky and thought about his friends. And thought of the good times they'd had. He was going to think about them as often as he could, in case one day, when he was old, he forgot everything. He reached up and took his mother's hand, and held it tight.

ACKNOWLEDGMENTS

Thank you to so many folks. Anyone who has obtained and read anything I've ever put out, a big ol' Thank you.

Special Thanks To: Dead Sky (Steve Wands, Kristy Baptist, Anna Kubik and Jeremy Wagner and team members I may have never mingled with in the real but are no less important) To all my family members. To nurses and elder care workers, we think we know about strength, but these folks...

Special peer shout outs: My heart beats faster for: Robert Ford, Chad Lutzke, Mercedes Yardley, Kelli Owen, Mike Lombardo, Jacob Haddon, Chris Enterline, Eric LaRocca, Josh Rountree, Brennan LaFaro, Todd Keisling, Ronald Kelly, Bridgett Nelson, Josh Malerman, Patrick Freivald, Kevin Lucia, Royal Poff, Somer Canon, Norman Prentiss, Tommy Clark, Candace Nola, Judith Sonnet, John Skipp, Jessica McHugh, and the rest my fellow writers who oft toil thanklessly in the same rubble as I.

ABOUT THE AUTHOR

John Boden was mostly raised in the mountains of Pennsylvania.

He is a bakery manager by trade and finds a regular sleep schedule overrated.

He currently resides with his beautiful wife and two sons, in a house sweetly haunted by the ghost of a beautician named, Darlene. He likes collecting lots of things and won't usually shut up about it. He believes Elvis is the King, Bigfoot is real and Midian is where the monsters live.

His writing is fairly well received and has been called unique of style

He's easy to track down either on Facebook or Twitter or some of them other high falutin' social media things.

OTHER BOOKS BY JOHN BODEN:

Dominoes

Jedi Summer

Spungunion

Walk The Darkness Down

Snarl

The Etiquette Of Booby Traps

With Chad Lutzke:

Out Behind The Barn

The Bedmakers

Wounds To Wishes

With Robert Ford:

Rattlesnake Kisses

Cattywampus

Wounds To Wishes